THE GREEK'S BOUGHT WIFE

BY
HELEN BIANCHIN

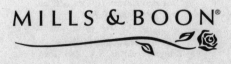

MILLS & BOON®

With sincere thanks to Samantha Bell

First published in Great Britain 2005
Harlequin Mills & Boon Limited,
Eton House, 18-24 Paradise Road, Richmond, Surrey TW9 1SR

© Helen Bianchin 2005

ISBN 0 263 84167 7

Set in Times Roman 10½ on 12½ pt.
01-0805-38100

Printed and bound in Spain
by Litografia Rosés, S.A., Barcelona

CHAPTER ONE

Nic Leandros eased the powerful Lexus down into the underground parking area beneath a luxurious apartment building located in Sydney's suburban Double Bay, slid into a reserved bay and cut the engine.

His cellphone rang, and he quickly checked the caller ID, uttered a husky oath, and let the call go to MessageBank.

Sabine…*again*. How many times had she called today? Four…five? The woman was becoming obsessive, he admitted with a wry grimace. He hadn't expected an easy end to the relationship. But how long would it take for Sabine to understand *no* meant precisely that?

It had been months since he'd cut the ties, politely refusing her veiled invitations until her protestations reached desperation point, whereupon he refused to take any of her calls. For the past several weeks she'd virtually stalked him, resorting to SMS text messaging several times a day and turning up wherever he happened to be…in his favoured Melbourne restaurants, at two parties and a fundraiser.

He'd issued a warning, followed it with legal action. Yet Sabine still persisted.

Nic crossed to the bank of lifts. He had no need to check the apartment number or the floor on which it was situated, for it was one of several owned by the Leandros Corporation and occupied until very recently by his young half-brother.

Sixteen years his junior, Vasili had been a much-loved addition to the Leandros family twenty-one years ago. To his father Paul, a delight, and the apple of Nicos' adored stepmother Stacey's eye.

Nic reflected on the affection they'd shared, despite the gap in their ages. Vasili's upbringing had followed an identical path to his own…strict and loving. How else could it be beneath Stacey's guiding hand?

Yet Vasili had developed a recklessness Nic had never aspired to. He'd sailed through scholastic studies, gained a degree in business management, and entered the Leandros Corporation at the bottom of the corporate ladder…as Nic had, succeeding without any seeming effort.

Vasili had remained in Sydney acquiring corporate skills, while Nic was based in the Melbourne head office, in between extensive travelling between America and Europe.

Yet their bond had remained a close one, despite the vagaries of distance.

Good-looking, fun, Vasili had had a love of life, girls, and fast cars…in that order.

Tragically, it had been the fast car—a Lamborghini—that caused Vasili's death little more than two weeks ago.

Nic had been aware of the numerous girls who sought Vasili's company, his bed, and his share of the Leandros fortune. Although Tina Matheson had been the first girl Vasili had invited to move in with him.

What Nic hadn't known was news of Tina's pregnancy. Stacey had been Vasili's only confidante in that piece of information, the day before his untimely death.

There had been no mention of it…hell, no visible sign of it as the slender auburn-haired girl had stood at Vasili's grave-side ten days ago.

Among the grief-stricken, Tina had stood apart. Cool, controlled, with a fragility he'd instinctively felt the need to ease.

Yet he'd been polite on introduction, distant as befitted the solemnity of the occasion, and had stood in silence as Stacey had issued Tina with an invitation to join the family in a private wake.

Tina's refusal had surprised him. Given the circumstances, he'd thought she'd use any advantage to further her relationship with the Leandros family.

If he was honest, he'd have admitted he wanted to see her again in less sombre surroundings, for there was some indefinable quality about her that intrigued him.

Her stance, the way she held herself aloof. The classical, fine-boned features, cream-textured skin. Eyes the colour and brilliance of emeralds, deep, unfathomable.

Untouchable, he'd reminded himself.

His half-brother's woman. The mother of Vasili's unborn child.

The existence of a Leandros grandchild had provided an element of hope for Paul and Stacey Leandros. The child of their child. A child who would share Vasili's inheritance, and take its rightful place in the Leandros family.

Both Paul and Stacey had assumed Tina would welcome their support, their help. Dammit, their unconditional affection and love.

Except Tina had politely refused Stacey's, then Paul's advances. Something that merely accelerated Stacey's grief to an inconsolable level.

Now it was Nic's turn to attempt to sway Tina's decision. *At any cost*, Paul had determined.

Money. Sufficient of it could buy most anything, anyone, Nic decided with wry cynicism as he passed through security and rode the lift to the penthouse level. Besides which, he was a shrewd judge of character, a lauded strategist…and he had a few contingency plans.

It was simply a matter of determining the one most likely to succeed, and putting it into action.

Seconds later he crossed the marble-tiled floor to a set of ornate double doors.

Nic pressed the call button, then held it down when no one answered.

Nic wondered at Vasili's fascination with the woman carrying his child, for at twenty-seven Tina was almost six years Vasili's senior, and the only child of a widowed mother whose remarriage five years ago had resulted in a move to Noosa on Queensland's Sunshine Coast.

Tina had a record of average scholastic achievements, a love of sport, life. A flair for fashion had led to a managerial position in an up-market Double Bay boutique owned by her mother. A collection of friends, but no long-term boyfriend.

Dammit, why didn't she answer?

Impatience creased his features as he withdrew his cellphone, hit auto-dial, and queried Paul as to when the apartment had last been checked.

His father's answer brought forth a frown. The morning following Vasili's death.

Two weeks ago?

'Given the current situation,' Paul relayed, 'Stacey refuses to interfere with Tina's live-in arrangement.' His voice sharpened. 'Give me a few minutes and I'll call you back.'

Nic didn't have to wait long for Paul to relay the building manager was on his way with a master-key.

The apartment offered stunning views over the bay, but Nic took little notice of the sparkling nightscape beyond floor-to-ceiling glass as he thanked the manager and closed the door behind him. Instead he walked through the lounge, eyes alert for any signs of occupation, only to discover there was none.

Vasili's clothes hung in one of two large walk-in robes, and there was an assortment of male toiletries atop a double marble vanity unit in the master *en suite*.

The sight of them hurt, like a stake through the heart. Curiously more so than when he'd received the tragic call from Paul; more so even than the funeral. For now there was the visual attestation Vasili would never return to claim what was his…clothes, possessions, or the joy of holding his child.

A muscle bunched at the edge of his jaw as he

crossed to the second robe, only to discover on open-ing the door that it was empty.

Nic moved through the apartment, checking a sec-ond bedroom, a third...and discovered both were empty. There were no clothes in either wardrobe or chest of drawers. No sign of any feminine possessions in each adjoining *en suite*.

A husky oath escaped from his lips.

Tina Matheson had moved out.

It was obvious Paul hadn't considered keeping tabs on her. Dammit, *he'd* only given the need a fleeting thought, then dismissed it, sure she'd milk the situa-tion, eagerly taking whatever Paul and Stacey offered. Hell, even demand more in a quest to set herself up for life by virtue of the child she carried.

He checked the dining-room, the kitchen, spotted a set of keys resting on the marble bench-top and reached for them, examining each before weighing the set in one hand. Then he slid them into his jacket pocket and made a phone call.

The name *Leandros* garnered respect. It also opened doors to data not easily available to the gen-eral public.

Within fifteen minutes Nic had the information he needed.

It didn't take long to drive the few kilometres to a small private hotel where Tina Matheson was regis-tered as a guest.

Locating her room took mere minutes, and when there was no answer to his knock he repeated the ac-tion, harder, more forceful than before.

He was about to give it another try when the security chain was removed, the lock disengaged, the door opened sufficiently for him to glimpse a female clutching a large bath-towel around her slender form.

Nic registered damp auburn curls piled high on her head, pale features, and a pair of brilliant emerald-green eyes.

Eyes that hardened somewhat as they ascertained his identity.

'Go away.'

The door slammed shut, and he stifled a lurid oath.

'Do that again,' he warned with dangerous silkiness, 'and I'll disregard common courtesy.'

He heard the security chain engage, then the door opened a fraction. 'I could take that as a threat and call the police.'

'Go ahead.'

'Don't tempt me.'

'Aren't you going to ask me in?'

'Not if I can help it.'

'We can have a conversation now,' Nic offered with deceptive mildness, 'in relative privacy. Or,' he paused slightly, 'I'll arrive at your place of business tomorrow and hold it there.'

There was a perceptible silence, then Nic heard the locks disengage, and the door swung open.

She was more petite than he recalled, but then she was barefoot. The bath-towel had been discarded in favour of a towelling robe.

She looked tired, and there were dark smudges beneath her eyes. The result of grief, lack of sleep...or both?

'Another Leandros emissary?' Tina took in the tall,

broad male frame clothed in superb tailoring, forced herself to meet and hold those dark, almost black eyes…and felt all her protective self-defence instincts rise to the fore.

'We have been introduced.'

The voice held a faint American-inflected drawl, and she suppressed a shiver of unease. Nic and Vasili Leandros might share the same father, but as men they were as chalk to cheese.

Whereas Vasili had borne an air of insouciant youth, Nic Leandros possessed an indefinable quality that meshed ruthlessness and power…and combined it with a sexual chemistry no woman could successfully ignore.

Raging hormones had to be the reason why she felt vaguely off balance. It couldn't be the man unsettling her.

'You want to conduct this conversation on the doorstep?'

Oh, Lord. She'd just emerged from the shower. 'You'll have to wait while I get dressed.' And she shut the door in his face.

It took only minutes to step into underwear, jeans, add bra and tee shirt. She didn't bother with her hair. As for make-up…forget it.

He was there when she pulled back the front door, his tall frame seeming even more threatening than before.

Men of Nic Leandros' ilk weren't used to having doors shut in their faces, she perceived with a certain wry humour as she silently indicated he could enter.

'Thank you.' His voice was dry, and held a degree of impatience as he followed her into the suite.

Tina turned to face him, aware of the need to take control.

'Let's get this over with, shall we?'

One eyebrow rose, and his gaze remained steady. 'Dispense with polite conversation?'

She lifted a hand and smoothed back a wayward fall of hair, only to silently damn the visible indication her nerves were twisting every which way but loose.

'Why pretend civility when we have opposing agendas?' Tina queried, and saw those dark eyes harden fractionally.

'Can you blame Stacey and my father for wanting to share a part of their grandson or granddaughter's life?' he queried quietly.

'Do you think I don't know where this is leading?'

'Enlighten me.'

'Let's see.' She tilted her head and began listing probable possibilities. 'What comes next? Any minute soon you'll present several attractive reasons why I should agree to your parents' desire to assign the Leandros name to Vasili's child.' She paused and drew in a deep breath.

Nic Leandros dominated the room, his presence a compelling entity that disturbed her more than she was prepared to admit.

'If I agree, the heat will be on for it to be raised and educated according to Leandros tradition.'

'And that's a problem…*because*?'

He didn't get it. 'I'll lose control.'

'Any decisions made will, of course, be reached by mutual agreement.'

'Oh, please.' Tina raked his features with evident cynicism. 'Give me a break.' Her gaze speared his. 'How long will it take your parents to lodge an *unfit parent* complaint after the birth?' She closed her eyes, then opened them. 'Deny that's the master plan.'

A muscle tensed at the edge of his jaw. 'I doubt anything of the sort has entered Stacey's mind.'

'But it will, eventually.'

Her fierceness and her fragility were a contradiction in terms, something he found intriguing.

'When I return to work and put the babe into a day-care nursery?' She felt as if she were on a runaway train. 'Employ sitters on the rare occasion I feel the need to socialise?'

'It's my parents' intention to provide handsomely for the child's welfare.' He waited a beat. 'The ball is in your court. Name your terms.'

'And they'll be met?' She lifted a hand and ran it wearily over her hair. 'Thanks, but no, thanks.'

He'd tabled each stumbling block and had a strategy for every one of them. It was just a matter of time... 'Perhaps you'd care to elaborate why?'

'I don't see how a one-night stand qualifies the right for the child to assume its deceased father's name.' If she'd hoped to shock, she gained no visible reaction from his expression. 'Especially when I had no intention of making it my own.'

Nic's eyes became hooded. 'Vasili meant nothing to you?'

Tina took her time with the question. 'We played

the boyfriend/girlfriend game.' She paused fractionally. 'It was…convenient. For each of us.' She had no obligation to relay *why*.

'The age difference didn't bother you?'

Her chin tilted a little and her eyes acquired a dangerous gleam. 'Are you implying Vasili was my *toy boy*? We were *friends*.'

'Yet you moved in with him.'

Explanations tended to become complicated. Yet Nic Leandros was entitled. How else would her decision make any sense?

'I sold my apartment,' Tina defended. 'I was in negotiations to buy another. Vasili suggested I move in with him instead of securing a hotel room or renting short-term.' It had seemed so logical at the time, and she'd insisted on contributing towards food and utilities.

'And shared his bed,' Nic accorded in a hateful drawl.

Her chin tilted a little, and her eyes blazed green fire. 'Once.'

Dammit, that was all it took. *Once.* A little too much champagne, a friendly kiss that had become more, and somehow they'd ended up in the same bed.

She dimly remembered voicing a half-hearted protest as instinctive wisdom had fought against the persuasiveness of Vasili's mouth, his hands. Then it had been too late. The sex had been less than noteworthy. Not that she'd had much experience to compare it with.

All the pent-up emotion of the past few weeks caught up with her. 'I should disillusion your mother…sorry, stepmother?' she offered the correction. 'Your father? Paint a false picture of a relationship that was only *friendship*?' She was on a roll, unable to stop. 'Enlighten them that the conception of their coveted grandchild was a mistake? Dammit,' she said forcefully, 'a meaningless, *forgettable* mistake.' She wanted to hit something, throw something. Anything to rid the impossible anger that burned within…at herself, for being so senseless.

'Obviously there were no precautions taken.'

Tina heard the words, and only just refrained from hitting the man who uttered them. *'Obviously.'*

'Yet you've taken no steps to abort the foetus.'

She drew in a sharp breath and pressed a protective hand to her waist. 'No.'

Nic's eyes narrowed. 'Would you have, if my parents had been unaware of the pregnancy?'

Tina didn't hesitate. 'No.'

The insistent ring of a cellphone sounded loud in the silence of the room, and Tina watched as he withdrew the unit, checked the caller ID, and registered his irritation as he thrust the cellphone back into his jacket pocket.

'Have you eaten?'

Her eyes widened. 'Excuse me?'

'Dinner.' His voice held an element of impatience.

He was talking of *food*? 'I don't see that's a relevant question.'

'It's relevant if you haven't eaten.'

'Why?'

'I'm suggesting we share a meal.'

'Again…*why*?'

She irritated and fascinated him at the same time. She was also the first woman in a long time to refuse his invitation.

'Go change. I'll make a reservation.'

Tina closed her eyes, then opened them and shot him a fierce glare. 'Are you usually this dictatorial?'

He extracted his cellphone, and hit a speed-dial button. 'I'm known to get what I want.'

'Really?' She was singularly unimpressed. And remained so at the ease with which he secured a table.

Nic regarded her steadily. 'You want to argue with me?'

'Heaven forbid any female would dare,' Tina offered facetiously, and caught a glimpse of something that was almost humour in those dark eyes.

'You being an exception?'

'Count on it.' She glared at him, then she crossed to the door. 'I want you to leave.'

His expression remained unchanged, except there was a sense of innate power, a strength of will, evident beneath the surface.

Her gaze arrowed in on his, and didn't waver. She could feel her spine stiffen...literally. 'I don't want to share a meal with you.'

'Same destination,' Nic stated. 'Separate cars.'

'That's a persuasive ploy?'

'A compromise. It's almost seven, neither of us have eaten, and we've yet to reach a satisfactory resolution.'

'*My* decision is made.'

'One that concerns *you*. However, there's a child's

life at stake. Your child.' He paused slightly. 'But indisputably also my brother's child.'

She *was* hungry. In the past few days she'd developed a heightened sensitivity to the smell of food. The thought of ordering a meal of her choice that she didn't need to prepare or cook was enticing. Besides, it was clear Nic Leandros wouldn't let up any time soon.

'Go wait outside while I change.'

'And have you lock the door behind me?' His expression held wry cynicism. 'Collect what clothes you need and get dressed in the *en suite*.'

She wanted to kill him…or at best do him physical harm. Yet it was no contest. A venue they drove to in separate cars was preferable to the intimacy of a hotel suite.

At least she'd be free to walk out of a restaurant undeterred. Whereas *here* it would be a different matter entirely. And, while his presence was unlikely to pose a threat, she had the distinct feeling he'd play any game by his own rules.

'There's a problem?'

Tina sent him a scathing glare. 'I'm deciding what method I should use to render you physical harm.'

His mouth quirked in silent amusement, and she bit back an attempt at childish retaliation as she crossed to the storage unit.

With quick, economical movements she collected black silk evening trousers, an emerald green silk camisole, matching jacket, and headed for the *en suite*.

A few minutes, minimum make-up, a vigorous

brush through her hair, and she was done. When she emerged it took only seconds to step into stiletto heels, then transfer money and keys into an evening purse.

Tina was conscious of his appraisal, and deliberately arched an eyebrow. 'Shall we leave?'

They rode the lift down to the basement car park, and within minutes Tina followed Nic's black Lexus to the trendy heart of Double Bay, parked, then accompanied him into a small, intimate restaurant filled with patrons.

The *maître d'* greeted Nic with the obsequious fervour reserved for a favoured patron, personally escorted them to a table, saw them seated and summoned the drink steward.

Prestigious, known for its fine cuisine, and expensive, Tina acknowledged as she cast the room a casual glance.

The service was excellent, and she requested mineral water, chose a starter as a main meal, and settled back in her chair.

The steward brought their drinks, served them with deferential good humour, then retreated.

'You eat here often.' It was a statement, not a query, and Nic subjected her to a solemn appraisal.

'Whenever I'm in Sydney.'

Uh-huh. The Leandros corporation had its main base in Melbourne. Vasili's parents resided there. So did Nic, Vasili had relayed...in between business trips to New York, London, Athens and Rome.

'I imagine you'll acquaint your parents with my decision?'

He fingered the stem of his wine goblet with deliberate distraction. 'When we're done with it.'

She held his gaze. 'There is no *when*.'

'What if I were to suggest an alternative option?' Nic paused, then added, 'Or two.'

She took a sip of icy liquid. 'There are none.'

'Adoption,' he presented with deceptive mildness. 'For a mutually agreed sum.'

Tina froze, temporarily unable to utter so much as a word for several long seconds before anger ignited and threatened to explode. 'You have to be joking.'

'One million dollars.'

She opened her mouth, then closed it again as she found her voice. 'Go to hell,' she managed in a fierce undertone as she collected her evening purse and stood to her feet.

'Two million.'

Tina registered the calmness apparent in his voice, and barely controlled the urge to throw something at him.

'Three.'

Incredulity was uppermost. She turned, only to come to a halt as her arm was caught in a firm grasp. She directed him a vehement glare that would have felled a lesser man. 'Let me go!'

His eyes held hers, their expression impossible to read. 'Sit down. Please,' he added with chilling softness. 'There are other options.'

'I don't see how you can top it,' Tina ventured savagely.

'Marriage.' He paused fractionally. 'To me.'

For a few heart-stopping seconds she remained

transfixed with shock. It took her time to find her voice. 'Are you *insane*?'

She picked up the glass and tossed the contents at him in a wildly spontaneous action, watching as he dodged the icy mineral water, and saw it hit his shoulder and cascade down his jacket, his shirt.

In the next instant the glass slipped from her fingers, hit the table, and slid onto the tiled floor to splinter into countless shards.

Tina was vaguely aware of the steward's presence, his concern, the removal of glass and mopping up operation. She even recalled offering an apology.

And heard Nic's drawling explanation. 'It's not often a man receives such an unusual reaction to his marriage proposal.'

She was vaguely aware of the steward's effusive congratulations, and the news took wing and spread.

Somehow she was no longer standing, but seated opposite the arrogant, ruthless man who had, she strongly suspected, stage-managed precisely this scenario.

'Retract it, and do it *now*,' Tina said in a fierce undertone.

'A marriage mutually convenient to both of us,' Nic continued silkily. 'It will give Vasili's child legitimacy and a legal place within the Leandros hierarchy.'

Her voice dripped ice. 'Haven't you forgotten something?'

A cameraman appeared out of nowhere and a camera flash temporarily blinded her.

'I won't be a part of it.'

'No?' Nic ventured silkily. 'Be warned, I can be your friend...or your worst nightmare.'

CHAPTER TWO

SUDDENLY it all fell into place, and Tina hated him. Truly *hated* him.

'This is the ultimate manipulative manoeuvre, isn't it?'

Everything about the evening up to this point had been a farce. The child she carried was of prime importance. The *only* importance.

'A process of elimination.' His drawled admission caused the breath to catch in her throat.

'You thought I was a money-grubbing bitch with an eye to the main chance?' Anger tore at her control when he didn't answer. 'You bastard.' The accusation whispered silkily from her lips.

His expression didn't change, nor did his gaze waver from her own. 'It was a possibility I had to consider.'

Tina attempted a deep calming breath, and cursed softly when it had no effect whatsoever. 'Should I surmise you've also run a routine check?'

She had nothing to hide, except one incident on record. He couldn't have delved that far, surely?

'Private schooling, love of sport, father killed in an accident when you were seventeen.' He paused for a few seconds. 'Assaulted a year later by an intruder during a home invasion.'

Tina felt the colour leach from her face as she

fought to control the vivid image obliterating her vision. In an instant she was back there in her bedroom, home alone in the apartment she'd shared with her mother, waking to an unusual sound close by, scared out of her wits in the knowledge someone was in her room.

The guttural voice, the stale smell of unwashed clothing...one hard hand clamped over her mouth while the other tossed aside bedcovers and ripped the thin nightshirt from her body. She'd fought like a demon, lashing out with her feet, her hands...

Nine years had passed since that frightening night. She'd had therapy, learnt coping mechanisms and acquired combat skills.

Her determination to be a survivor not a victim had left her with an almost obsessive need for security measures, a mistrust of men...and a legacy of infrequent nightmares.

'Assaulted, but not raped,' Tina managed quietly. Although it had come close. Too close. He'd hurt her, broken her arm, fractured three of her ribs.

'You were hospitalised.'

So he'd gained access to the medical report.

'Did you also unearth a speeding ticket, a few parking violations?' She was like a speeding train, unable to stop. 'Run a check my taxes are paid to date?'

His steady gaze was unnerving as the silence stretched between them.

'I'm suggesting a marriage in name only,' Nic offered in a faintly accented drawl.

'A sham? Separate rooms, separate lives?'

'A mutually convenient partnership,' he elaborated. 'A shared social existence.'

'Isn't that taking familial duty and devotion just a little too far?'

'Vasili would want his child to be well cared for…to legitimately bear the Leandros name. I can at least do that for him.'

'Regardless of *my* wishes?'

'You'll be more than adequately compensated. Houses at home and abroad, frequent travel, jewellery, an extremely generous allowance.'

'For which I should be duly grateful?' If looks could kill, he'd fall dead on the spot. 'And *you*?' Tina demanded. 'What would you get out of such a marriage?'

'A wife, a legitimate Leandros heir, a social partner.' He waited a beat. 'And one very persistent woman out of my life.'

'I very much doubt you need protection from anyone. Especially a woman!'

Tina was so impossibly angry she didn't pause to think. 'I imagine your wife would be expected to turn a blind eye to a mistress discreetly set up in an apartment somewhere?' She leaned forward and sharpened a mythical dart, just for the hell of it. 'Or does your taste run to same-sex lovers?'

She glimpsed something hard in the depths of those dark eyes, then it was gone.

'Are you done?'

Tina paid no heed to the dangerous silkiness in his voice. 'What about my needs?'

His eyes locked with hers, and she couldn't look away. 'All you have to do is ask.'

She swung her hand towards his face. Except it didn't connect.

Instead he used her momentum to pull her into his arms and silenced her by covering her mouth with his own in a kiss that tore her composure to shreds.

Nothing she'd ever experienced came close to the frankly sensual plundering he subjected her to. It was an invasion of the senses, a flagrant, devastating attempt to suppress her will.

When he released her she could barely stand, and she was hardly aware of the notes he tossed onto the table, or that he followed as she turned and walked from the restaurant.

It was impossible to ignore him, for he was *there* as she unlocked her Volkswagen...a funky bright yellow sedan, with a sunroof, that she'd fallen in love with on sight.

'Tomorrow,' Nic inclined as she slid in behind the wheel.

'Go to hell.' Fierce, angry, *foolish* words, she perceived as she fired the engine and sent the car towards the exit at a speed in excess of the marked restriction.

Nic Leandros was the most impossible man she'd ever met. If she never saw him again, it would be too soon.

A sharp horn-blast startled her, and she swore beneath her breath at her failure to notice the traffic light had changed from red to green.

Focus, Tina silently berated as she sent the car forward.

In a determined bid, she attempted to dismiss Nic Leandros from her mind.

Except it didn't work. She could still feel the pressure of his mouth on her own, the taste of him. Dammit, the sensual sweep of his tongue.

Oh, for heaven's sake! *Get over it.*

Nic Leandros was merely exerting male dominance in a spontaneous attempt to still her angry tirade.

Tina slept badly, and woke feeling as if she'd run a marathon. The beginnings of a headache threatened an emergence, and her stomach didn't feel as if it belonged to her at all.

Sweet tea and dry toast…or was that merely an old wives' tale?

The temptation to bury her head beneath the pillow and tell the world to go away was uppermost. Except it wasn't going to happen.

There was work…and some time during the day she had to face Nic Leandros. The hope *he* might go away was as unlikely to be realised as a snowfall in summer.

What time was it? She checked the digital clock and groaned. Another hour before room service would deliver breakfast.

Okay, so she could do the sweet tea, and there was probably a snack-pack of dry biscuits in the complimentary mini-bar. The day's newspaper should already be outside her door…

If her stomach decided to revolt, better sooner than later, she determined a trifle grimly.

Ten minutes later she cast the newspaper aside and took a leisurely shower, then dressed; she ate a healthy breakfast, tidied the suite, then she cast a glance at the time.

It was early, yet the need to keep occupied prompted the thought of work. Better to be at the boutique than sit twiddling her thumbs in a hotel room.

She would dust the fittings, vacuum, then check the floor stock before opening up at the usual time.

Early mornings tended to be slow, with few patrons making an appearance much before ten, when Lily reported in for the day.

With that in mind she collected her laptop, caught up her bag and went down to collect her car.

Double Bay was only a matter of kilometres distant, and she parked at the rear of the building, activated the car alarm, then crossed to the entrance out front.

Tina took great pride in the boutique with its elegant salon, beyond which lay a small back room where extra stock was stored, as well as the usual utilities.

There was a need to be in familiar surroundings, she acknowledged as she crossed the salon. To *think* and rationalise Nic Leandros' proposition. She'd be damned if she'd term it a *proposal*.

She hadn't thought of children; she definitely hadn't considered marriage.

It was the reason she socialised within the safe company of a few selected and trusted friends. Vasili used to tease that while *he* protected her from male predators, *she* protected him from female fortune hunters. A mutually satisfactory relationship.

At least it had been until that fateful night when a friendly kiss had led to more. A tenderly concerned

Vasili who had suggested it was time she made the final leap to sexual intimacy with a friend for whom she held affection and trust. Add the enhancement of wine…and it had seemed so *logical* at the time.

Ironic that the act should result in pregnancy. Yet she wanted this child…an unexpected gift in living memory of a fun and caring young man.

Was she right in keeping the child solely *hers*? If Vasili were alive, they'd share parenting and the child would assume the Leandros name.

So why did she baulk at Nic Leandros' proposition?

Because Vasili's half-brother was an unknown quantity. Older, ruthless…*dangerous*.

Yet she had to concede there were advantages. The child would have a father figure, a legal right to its heritage, grandparents, *family*. A stable, loving environment in which to grow.

On a personal level she'd have a steady male companion whom she could trust not to hit on her at the end of an evening.

Another plus was the knowledge Nic travelled extensively on business. A lot of the time he wouldn't be in the same city, the same country.

The vacuum hummed as she ran it over carpet and marble tiles, then she carefully smoothed a dusting cloth over shelving, polished the mirrors before standing back to admire her handiwork.

The salon held the restrained elegance of an upmarket boutique, its design and fittings…so exactly right for the Double Bay location renowned for its fashionistas, the wealthy women who could indulge their expensive tastes in imported and Australian designer apparel.

Tina possessed a natural love of clothes, and had done so for as long as she could remember, mix and matching outfits as she'd dressed her dolls...Barbie, of course, in each of her guises. As a teenager, she'd helped out in her mother's boutique, proving she had a keen eye for fashion, accessories, and an instinctual flair for putting things together.

There was no hesitation in which field she'd make her career, and she'd learnt the retail clothing trade from the floor up...initially through her mother's expert tutelage, then in one of Sydney's large city stores for three years before returning to co-manage her mother's Double Bay boutique.

Until five years ago when Claire had met and married Felipe, the second love of her life, shifted base to Noosa, leased her apartment and left Tina in control.

The Double Bay social set employed a reasonably routine shopping pattern, meeting around nine-thirty for coffee, electing to begin browsing the various boutiques around ten-thirty, followed by a long lunch at one of the trendy restaurants, before doing the air-kiss thing and departing for homes cleaned by professionals.

Lily arrived promptly at ten, almost bursting into the boutique, modifying her excitement as Tina finished dealing with a patron who'd bought the entire outfit displayed in the front window...including shoes and handbag.

A folded newspaper was placed onto the glass-topped island counter.

'Have you *seen* this?' Lily demanded, *sotto voce*, following it with an irrepressible grin.

Tina glanced at the newsprint and felt the breath catch in her throat. Strategically placed centre page was a reasonably sized photograph taken the previous night at the restaurant, together with a bold caption speculating a date for Nic Leandros' forthcoming marriage to Tina Matheson.

'How come you kept this to yourself?' Lily teased. *'Give.'*

The truth was a credibility stretch...even for a friend. 'It represents a gross misinterpretation by the media.' Initiated by a determined manipulative man, Tina added silently, and met Lily's speculative gaze.

'That's all you're going to say?'

'For now.'

The electronic door buzzer provided a timely interruption, and she turned to discover the courier delivery guy with a packing box.

'Where do you want this?'

Three patrons entered the boutique, one serious buyer, Tina judged, and two browsers idly riffling through the racks.

With a quick word she excused herself and crossed to the courier's side. 'Out back.' She silently signalled Lily to take over while she checked the invoice.

Minutes later the courier clipped the signed invoice onto his clipboard and departed, leaving Tina to cross to the two women checking out a garment, whereupon she offered assistance, complimenting the designer, the fabric and style.

Another sale, followed soon after by another, adding to a productive morning, Tina reflected as she took a moment to complete the unpacking of new stock.

'Oh, my.'

The hushed tone in Lily's voice had Tina shooting a glance in her direction. 'As in?'

'Serious eye candy about to walk through the door.'

Male, Tina deduced. An attractive husband intent on buying his wife an expensive gift? She didn't bother glancing up. 'Go for it.'

'I wish.'

Lily's reverence brought forth a slight smile. Lily was equally *friend* as valued employee, and considered herself to be a connoisseur of men.

'However, he's *yours*.'

Tina's gaze shifted to the salon entrance and the breath caught in her throat in recognition of the man engaging Lily in conversation.

Nic Leandros…*here*?

If he thought she'd walk over to him and play *pretend* in Lily's presence, he could think again.

With outward calm Tina extracted the last garment from the box, deftly inserted a clothes hanger and transferred it onto a rack so it could air for a while. After lunch she'd freshen today's delivery with the steam-iron before transferring the garments onto display racks in the salon.

She was acutely aware of the muted background music whispering through strategically placed speakers, creating a relaxed ambience that was reflected in the elegant combination of delicately blended cream, wheat and beige utilised in the furnishings. A luxurious setting to display the exclusive range of designer garments for which the boutique was known.

'Tina.'

It was a voice she'd recognise anywhere. It was also one she didn't want to hear. Yet good manners forced her to school her features into a polite mask as she turned to face Nic Leandros.

Her gaze was silently challenging. 'Is there something I can help you with?' Cool...she could do *cool*, despite the fact her nervous system was in direct conflict. It was insane the way one glance at that well-shaped, sensual mouth brought a vivid recall of how it had felt possessing her own.

'Lunch,' Nic informed her with deceptive calm. 'Your assistant is happy to take charge for an hour.'

He really was the limit! 'I already have plans.' She didn't, but he wasn't to know that.

'Change them.'

'Why should I do that?'

'We can discuss arrangements here,' he informed steadily. 'Or over lunch. Choose.'

The electronic door buzzer sounded, signalling the arrival of a client.

'This is neither the time nor the place,' Tina protested quietly, silently hating him for placing her in such an invidious position. She made an instant decision. 'Give me five minutes.'

She made it in four, spoke briefly to Lily, preceded him from the boutique, and waited until they reached the pavement before demanding, 'What do you want?'

She kept her voice low, but her pent-up anger was an audible force.

'To continue the discussion you walked out on last night.'

His drawled tone held a steely quality she chose to ignore. 'You're giving me a choice?'

There were a few trendy cafés and restaurants dotting the street, and Nic indicated one close by.

She wanted to turn and retrace her steps, and almost did. Except he'd probably follow.

Within seconds he caught a waiter's attention, sought a table, and waited until they were seated before venturing, 'It's possible the media will make contact with you at some stage this afternoon.'

Tina was unable to prevent a cynical element tinging her voice. 'For this I need your help?'

Nic's gaze remained steady. 'Regarding my statement announcing our imminent marriage.'

A waitress crossed to their table and stood with pen and pad poised as Nic placed an order for two.

'I may not *want* the chicken Caesar salad,' Tina stated, and fixed Nic a deliberate glare before turning towards the waitress. 'Don't you just hate it when a man thinks he knows a woman's mind?' A double-edged query, if ever there was one.

The waitress, having undoubtedly witnessed the behaviour of numerous patrons during her employment, merely flicked Tina a glance that clearly queried Tina's sanity.

What woman wouldn't give her eye-teeth to have a man of Nic Leandros' ilk appear so...in control?

Damn. She liked Caesar salad. 'Make mine spinach

and fetta tortellini with the mushroom and bacon sauce.'

Tina met Nic's hooded gaze. 'We can argue this back and forth for ever.' She wanted to hit him…or, failing that, go several rounds in verbal battle. 'Give me one good reason why I should agree to marry you, aside from being pregnant with Vasili's child.'

He regarded her thoughtfully. 'Protection.' He could promise her that. 'Loyalty. Trust,' he endorsed quietly.

Sans love or fidelity.

Get real, a silent voice taunted. Neither love nor fidelity enter the equation. Nor do you want them to. So why even go there?

'And the child? You intend claiming it as your own?'

Nic's eyes narrowed. 'Foster the illusion I'm the child's biological father?'

Her chin tilted a little. 'Yes.'

'I will delight in my wife's pregnancy, and initiate adoption proceedings immediately following the birth.'

Ensuring the legalities were neatly taken care of.

'You avoided answering the question.'

'The child will be born a legitimate Leandros, with two parents.' His eyes speared hers. 'No one, apart from Paul and Stacey, need know personal details.'

'And Claire.' Dear heaven, she had yet to enlighten her mother of the pregnancy. She eyeballed the man seated opposite. 'I won't keep the truth from her.'

'I wasn't going to suggest you do.'

There were a few other conditions she needed to

voice, and she paused as the waitress presented their meals.

'Claire's boutique is my responsibility,' Tina insisted as soon as the waitress was out of earshot. 'Don't expect me to give up work and assume a social butterfly persona.'

'No objection, with one proviso.' Dark eyes lanced her own. 'Unless the medics advise otherwise.'

She wanted to argue, and her eyes darkened to a deep emerald-green. Something that fascinated him. She was fire and ice, and a complex mix of strength and vulnerability.

'I want a prenuptial agreement protecting my interests.'

That was his criterion, surely? 'Anything else?'

'What if either one of us chose to file for divorce?'

'I doubt the possibility will occur.'

'But if it does?' Tina persisted, and met his hard, level look.

'Be aware I'd fight you in court to assume full custody of the child.'

'You'd never get it,' she said with certainty. 'The courts generally favour the mother, especially when the male parent is not even the child's biological father.'

One eyebrow arched in silent cynicism. 'You doubt my ability to prove a case against you?'

A chill shiver feathered its way down her spine. Nic Leandros had both wealth and power in his favour. Sufficient of both to employ the finest legal brains in the country.

'No.' She paused imperceptibly. 'But don't under-estimate my determination to oppose you.'

Brave words from a brave woman. He selected his cutlery and indicated she should do the same. 'Let's eat, shall we?'

The tortellini looked and smelt delicious, but Tina's appetite had gone on strike. Instead, she cast an en-vious glance at the crisp cos lettuce in Nic's bowl, the croutons and sliced chicken, the delicate sauce…and caught the faintly humorous twist at the edge of his mouth.

Without a word he signalled the waitress, ordered another chicken Caesar salad, and met Tina's glare with equanimity.

'What do you think you're doing?'

'Ensuring you have what you'd prefer to eat.'

Her glare intensified. 'And you know this *because*?'

One eyebrow rose. 'Can I look forward to a battle-field with every meal we share?'

'Count on it if you intend overriding every choice I make!'

Nevertheless the Caesar salad, when it arrived, was too tempting to resist, and she ate in silence while steadfastly ignoring the man seated opposite.

'No polite conversation?'

Tina offered him a level glance. 'I was trying to avoid indigestion.'

His soft laughter surprised her, and her eyes wid-ened fractionally as she caught a gleam of humour in those dark eyes.

'Our relationship will be an interesting one.'

His drawled observation attacked her equilibrium,

and she fought to retain it. 'A qualification…I've yet to agree.'

'But you will.'

'Why so sure?'

'Because in your heart you know Vasili would see our liaison as an ideal solution.'

It didn't help Nic Leandros was right. 'Together with your assurance the alternative isn't something I'd want to contemplate?'

He took his time. 'Precisely.'

Tina wanted to throw something at him, and almost did. 'I don't like threats.'

'Believe it's a statement of fact.'

The icy certainty in his voice was a vivid reminder she didn't stand a chance against the wealth and influence of the Leandros family.

This…*marriage*, Tina qualified, was merely a business arrangement, with advantages for her, a child who surely *deserved* a stable upbringing…as opposed to a tug-of-war custody battle.

She didn't want to give in. Especially to this man, whose powerful presence disturbed her more than she was prepared to admit.

Yet a marriage based on mutual convenience among the wealthy wasn't so unusual. It forged a legal partnership, built wealth and provided heirs. A beneficial arrangement, legally documented and containing clearly defined boundaries.

'I want everything in writing.' She rose to her feet and sent him a long direct look. 'Subject to my legal advisor's perusal and approval.'

Nic followed her actions, extracted notes from his

wallet and tossed them on the table. 'The document will be delivered to you by courier late this afternoon. A copy of which will be despatched to your lawyer.' He waited a beat. 'Whose name is?'

Tina gave it, and battled the apprehension curling deep inside.

An instinctive omen? Don't be ridiculous, she silently derided as she made her way out of the restaurant. This isn't personal…it's business.

She paused as she reached the pavement. 'We'll be in touch.' Then she turned and walked away from him without so much as a backwards glance.

Outward composure, when inwardly her nerves were threatened to shred into a tangled mess.

Lily could barely contain her curiosity as Tina re-entered the boutique. 'Details,' Lily begged without preamble.

Truth wasn't an option, so she went with ambiguity. 'We're still working them out.'

A call from her lawyer a few hours later insisting on a personal consultation at day's end didn't surprise her. Nor, as she sat opposite him, did his cautionary advice.

He agreed, however, that each of her concerns had been adequately dealt with from a business aspect.

Tina signed, her signature was duly witnessed, and she walked out into the cool evening air, aware she'd just sealed her fate.

An hour later her cellphone rang, and she discovered Nic Leandros on the line.

'I've arranged an intimate ceremony at the weekend

in my home, immediate family only.' He barely paused. 'Any further media queries, refer them to me.'

Her heart leapt into her throat. 'So soon?'

'Why delay?'

She closed her eyes, then opened them again. *Because I'm not ready for this.* But then it was doubtful she'd *ever* be ready.

CHAPTER THREE

THE following few days passed in a blur of activity as Tina dealt with everything that needed to be done.

First and foremost had been a lengthy call to her mother, together with a wedding invitation.

Work became a welcome distraction as she fielded media enquiries, perused and signed relevant paperwork, and applied considerable effort towards choosing something suitable to wear on *the day*.

A day that came around far too quickly for her peace of mind, and one that began with a leisurely shared breakfast with Claire and Felipe at their hotel. Followed at her mother's insistence by a pampering session, massage, lunch, facial, hair treatment…the works.

A thoughtful gesture, gifted with the intention of helping her relax and unwind, after which they returned to Claire and Felipe's hotel suite in order to change and drive to Nic's Rose Bay home.

Tina had chosen an ivory silk dress with a beautifully crafted bodice, spaghetti straps, whose skirt was a dream in layered chiffon. There was a stylish matching ivory silk jacket. Stiletto heels in matching ivory completed the outfit, and she added an emerald drop pendant and ear-studs.

A small intimate family wedding involved Stacey and Paul Leandros, Claire and Felipe, the celebrant, together with the bride and groom, and was held in the large study of Nic's elegant Rose Bay home.

A setting that added formality to the occasion as Tina stood at Nic's side.

The wide diamond-encrusted wedding ring felt strange on her finger, and she hid her surprise as Nic held out a gold band for her to slide onto his finger. Somehow it seemed an unexpected gesture, given the nature of their union.

So too was the brush of his lips to her cheek…until she registered the camera flash and realised both Stacey and Claire had taken photos.

Afterwards there was champagne, which she declined, and she sipped something light and innocuous as she stood beside the tall, immaculately suited man who was now her husband.

It was too late for second thoughts…and, heaven knew, she had plenty! Such as where was her sanity when she agreed to become Tina *Leandros*.

Already she was playing the *pretend* game. So too, she observed, was everyone else in the elegant lounge room.

Nic, because he'd achieved his objective. Stacey and Paul, for now the child of the son they'd had together would legitimately become part of the Leandros family. Claire, because she loved her daughter and wanted only for Tina to be in a caring relationship.

Claire, the eternal optimist, who undoubtedly held the hope *care* would develop into affection and become *love*.

As if that were going to happen!

'Shall we leave?' Nic suggested smoothly, and received murmurs of assent.

Dinner at an exclusive city restaurant where the façade would continue, Tina accorded. Although was it a façade? Claire and Stacey seemed to have struck up a friendship, and Felipe appeared at ease in Paul and Nic's company.

In hindsight it was a pleasant evening. The venue, the food were superb; so too was the service.

Nic had inherited his father's genes, for both men shared a similar height and breadth of shoulder. There was a camaraderie between them, an equality and evident respect.

Apparent, too, was the love Paul had for his wife. It was there in the way he smiled, the light touch of his hand, the gleaming depth in his eyes.

To an onlooker their tableau would appear a convivial gathering of three couples who were very good friends.

Which simply went to show appearances were deceptive, for who would guess the bride and groom were barely acquainted, or that until this evening each set of parents had never met?

It was late when they left the restaurant, parted with affection, and went their separate ways.

Nic unlocked the Lexus, saw Tina seated, then walked round to slide in behind the wheel. Within seconds he fired the engine and eased the car into the flow of traffic.

'Nothing to say?'

Tina cast his profile a measured look. In the semi-darkness of the car's interior his facial features were all angles and planes.

'I'm all talked out.'

'That bad?'

Bad didn't work for her, for the evening had been superficially pleasant. Except she'd been all too aware of the well-hidden undercurrents associated with the marriage and its celebration.

'Everything was absolutely fabulous.' She transferred her attention to the scene beyond the windscreen, focusing on the well-lit street and the cars traversing it.

'Definitely overkill.'

Did his voice hold a tinge of humour, or was it just her imagination?

The day began to catch up with her...the trepidation, doubts, together with several nights of insufficient sleep. It became almost impossible to keep her eyes open, and after a few minutes she didn't even try.

Tina recalled stirring, and settling into a more comfortable position...then nothing as she sank into deep, dreamless slumber.

When she woke sunlight was edging through the wooden shutters, and for a few seconds she had no idea where she was. Then memory returned, and with it the knowledge she was in a large bed in the suite Nic had allocated her in an upstairs wing of his home.

The first shock was registering the time...the next, becoming aware she'd been divested of her clothes, with the exception of bra, briefs, tights and half-slip.

Dammit, he must have carried her indoors and put her to bed.

Great. So much for personal privacy.

Shower, dress, something to eat, then she'd be out the door and on her way to Double Bay…in less than an hour. Hopefully without encountering Nic Leandros.

She almost made it. Would have if she hadn't encountered Nic in the kitchen about to pour what was presumably his second coffee for the morning.

'Sleep well?'

No one had the right to look so darn good at this hour. Freshly shaven, hair groomed, dark trousers, blue shirt and dark blue tie, suit jacket loosely folded over the back of a chair: Nic projected an enviable aura of power.

Tina sent him a telling look. 'You should have woken me last night, instead of putting me to bed.'

'You don't believe I tried?'

'Not hard enough.'

She hadn't stirred once…as he'd lifted her from the car, carried her upstairs, nor when he'd laid her down onto the bed and carefully removed her shoes and outer clothes. Tiredness related to pregnancy?

He indicated the carafe. 'Coffee?'

The aroma teased her senses, taunted her with anticipation of how it would taste, and she shook her head. 'Can't have caffeine.'

His gaze narrowed fractionally as he took in her pale features, the dark smudges beneath her eyes.

'You'll find several blends of tea in the pantry.' He

swept a hand towards the refrigerator. 'Fix whatever you want to eat.'

'Don't have time.' Memo to self: unearth or buy an alarm clock.

His gaze sharpened. 'Make time.'

Tina rolled her eyes. 'I'll grab some fruit and yoghurt when I open the boutique.'

'Ensure you do.'

She offered a mock salute. 'Yessir.'

Sassy...definitely sassy, Nic decided.

He drained his coffee, caught up his suit jacket and shrugged into it, then collected his laptop.

'I'll be in Melbourne all day. Don't wait dinner.' He indicated a set of keys and two modems on the table. 'Yours. Security codes to the house, garage, gates.' His cellphone rang, and he checked caller ID and rejected the call. 'I employ staff to take care of the house and gardens.' He turned towards the door. 'Have a good day.'

Tina watched his departing form, drew in a deep breath and released it slowly.

Married one day, and flung abruptly into reality the next.

What did you expect?

Nothing, absolutely nothing.

A quick glance at the time spurred her into action, and five minutes later she slid into her car, eased it free of the driveway and took the street leading to the main arterial road.

Traffic at this hour was at a peak, and, although Double Bay was only two suburbs distant, it was a few minutes past nine when she unlocked the boutique.

Food was a priority, and hot sweet tea. The small bar fridge out back held a few tubs of yoghurt, a few apples and bananas, and Tina snacked in between setting up.

Lily arrived early, which was just as well, for the day became extremely busy.

Genuine interest for the clothes, or merely an opportunity to check out Nic Leandros' new wife?

Somehow Tina suspected it was the latter.

'Are you going to tell me?' Lily began when there was a brief lull. 'Or do I have to drag it out of you word by word?'

'The wedding?'

'Love the ring…definitely in the *ohmigod* range,' Lily accorded with an impish grin, then added sternly, 'I want every little detail.'

'Armani ensemble in ivory, killer heels.' Tina ticked each finger in turn. 'Celebrant, Nic's parents, mine. Followed by dinner in the city.'

'That's it?'

'Pretty much.'

'And?'

'There is no *"and"*.'

'Nic Leandros is one sexy-looking beast.'

In spades, Tina agreed silently, relieved at the sound of the electronic door buzzer.

'We're not done,' Lily warned *sotto voce* as she went forward to greet the two elegantly clad women who entered the salon.

Lunch was something she sent Lily out for, and

managed a ten-minute break in which to eat the chicken salad sandwich. Lily did likewise, foregoing her usual half-hour in order to help with the influx of customers.

Consequently by day's end all Tina wanted was a leisurely shower, dinner, followed by an early night.

'What *was* that?' Lily queried as Tina locked up and they walked to their respective cars. 'A day in the life of Nic Leandros' new bride?'

'Got it in one.'

'What's up, Tina?'

Lily's quiet sincerity brought a slight catch to her throat. 'I don't know what you mean.'

'Yes, you do,' Lily said gently. 'Just…I'm here for you if needed.'

Oh, dear heaven. She'd have to brush up her acting skills if Lily could sense not all was what it was purported to be!

'Thanks,' she managed gratefully. 'I'm fine. Really,' she added with a bright smile. *And cut,* a silent director ordered. Don't overdo it.

'Uh-huh.'

The truth was stranger than fiction, and not something she intended to divulge. Yet Lily was a friend, insightful, intuitive and caring.

'It's been a hectic, emotional week. Nic—' She almost added *Leandros*, and just stopped herself in time.

'Swept you off your feet?' Lily's grin was infectious.

'Yes.' She offered a smile of her own. 'And now I get to go home and play *wife*.'

'Like that's a hardship?'

It was a game, she justified as she eased the car from its parking space. All she had to do was maintain the pretence.

How difficult could it be?

Nic Leandros' home was situated in a tranquil tree-lined street where magnificent mansions of varying design and age offered the established luxury of wealth.

Tina released the ornate wrought-iron gates guarding entrance to the elegant structure ahead.

Set in sloping, immaculately kept grounds with a semi-circular driveway bordered by miniature topiary, the house itself was impressive. Double-storeyed, with cream-plastered walls, large timber-shuttered windows, a cream and terracotta tiled roof, the entrance gained via a set of large panelled double doors.

A four-car garage lay to the right, with an internal entry to the house.

Tina activated the module and the doors slid up to reveal a luxury Porsche SUV parked in one bay.

She parked alongside and cut the engine. The garage had been empty when she'd left this morning. A new acquisition? Had to be, she determined as she retrieved her laptop and crossed into the house.

Travertine marble floors, a wide curving staircase, exquisite light fittings, elegant furniture, large rooms... There was a formal lounge and dining-room plus informal dining area, kitchen, and utilities on the ground level. Five bedrooms, each with *en suite*, plus a master suite, large study and a private lounge on the upper level.

A row of French doors led from the formal lounge

and dining-room onto a large terrace, which offered magnificent harbour views. Wide steps led down to sculptured gardens and a beautifully designed infinity pool.

It was pleasant to be able to explore at her leisure. Yesterday hadn't offered much opportunity.

All her clothing had been unpacked and placed in the walk-in robe, folded in drawers, and suitcases presumably stored elsewhere. After a busy day and a particularly hectic week it came as a welcome surprise. No doubt due to the invisible household help.

A shower and change of clothes made her feel almost human again…and hungry, she realised as she made her way down to the kitchen.

A handwritten note signed by *Maria* was attached to the refrigerator door advising there was a cooked casserole ready to be heated.

Tina extracted a portion, heated it in the microwave and decided to eat out on the terrace.

The evening was clear, the sun's light diminishing as the deep orange orb sank slowly towards the horizon. In the distance street lights were beginning to spring on, and thè temperature cooled, turning the sparkling harbour waters to a dark, gun-metal grey.

There were ferries crossing towards Manly, fast hydrofoils carrying working passengers to the North Shore. A large tanker lay anchored way out past the Heads, and a passenger ship was being led in to berth by two tugboats.

Dusk fell and Tina collected her plate and returned indoors, locked up, and began switching on lights as she moved through to the kitchen.

The day's boutique sales were loaded onto computer disk ready for her to check through and assess stock.

A desk in her bedroom would be ideal, together with access to an internet connection. Nic's study? Not an option without his permission. Meantime the dining-room table would have to suffice.

Tina was still there when Nic walked into the room, and his gaze narrowed at the naked fear evident for a few shocking seconds before she successfully masked her expression.

He bit back a savage imprecation. 'In future I'll put a call through to your cellphone when I reach the gates.'

'Why?' she managed steadily. It had taken years of practice to recover her guard so quickly. 'You have state-of-the-art security. I doubt anyone could enter the house undetected. You have the tread of a cat,' she observed and tried for humour. 'So, next time whistle "Dixie".'

The edge of his mouth twitched at the implication. She was something else. He crossed to the coffee-maker and set it up. 'Busy day?'

'Polite conversation?'

Nic sent her a searching look. 'A simple enquiry.'

'The boutique was host to curiosity seekers bent on a discovery mission.'

He didn't pretend to misunderstand as he loosened his tie, and shrugged out of his jacket. 'That bothers you?'

'Sydney was Vasili's scene,' she clarified quietly.

'Now it has become mine.'

People would speculate why she'd partnered one brother, yet married the other. A fact that was already garnering interest.

So…she'd deal with it.

'How was your flight?'

Nic poured coffee into a cup, added sugar, and crossed to the table. 'Uneventful.'

His close proximity unsettled her. His choice of cologne was subtle, yet it stirred her senses. Blatant sensuality and elemental ruthlessness were a potent mix. Possessed of a steel-muscled body, broad sculptured facial features…the result was dynamite.

A force to be reckoned with, she added silently, aware just how indomitable he was to oppose.

What would he be like as a lover?

Dear God…*where had that thought come from*?

She couldn't *want* to find out, surely? The thought alone verged on insanity.

Hormones, she decided unsteadily. Had to be. Anything else was madness.

Tina quickly diverted her attention to the laptop. 'I'm almost done.' The sooner the better, then she could escape to her suite. 'There's a casserole in the fridge, courtesy of Maria, if you haven't eaten.' She keyed in the last of the data, pressed 'save', closed down and rose to her feet.

'I've accepted an invitation to dine with close family friends Thursday evening. Naturally you'll accompany me.'

She wanted to refuse, and almost did. Except declining wasn't really an option.

'It's a given,' he said quietly.

Was she that transparent? Without a further word she collected the laptop and vacated the room, unaware of the speculative expression in the man's dark eyes as he watched her go.

Surprisingly sleep came easily within minutes of sliding between the bedcovers, and she woke to the sound of her newly acquired alarm clock, rose, showered and dressed, only to discover the kitchen empty and Nic had already left for the day.

A day that was equally busy as the one preceding it, with good sales in accessories…women who were prepared to purchase in order to qualify a reason for checking out the Leandros' sole heir's new wife.

Don't knock it, a sage voice silently advised. Just smile sweetly and thank them for their patronage.

Tina's cellphone beeped with an incoming SMS message as she closed the boutique. *Business meeting. Home late. Nic.*

What did she expect? Company? Conversation?

Nic Leandros led a high-profile business life…even more so now, given he'd taken control of the Sydney office.

Hadn't she expressed silent relief at the thought she would hardly see him? So what was with the slight air of disappointment?

Get a grip.

She'd lived alone for several years and liked her solitary existence, as well as her ability to *choose* how she socialised and with whom. There was the boutique, her love of clothes, the constant striving to continue in Claire's footsteps and maintain one of the top-selling designer clothing boutiques in Double Bay.

She was providing her child with two parents and a brilliant future. What more could she ask?

CHAPTER FOUR

CHOOSING what to wear caused several indecisive minutes as Tina mentally selected and discarded clothes at random. Close family friends indicated a need for smart casual attire. Yet if they numbered among the social echelon, dressing to kill would be more appropriate.

She opted to go with a slim-fitting, classic black dress with a wide scooped neckline and black chiffon three-quarter ruched sleeves.

Make-up was understated, with emphasis on her eyes and warm pink gloss highlighting her lips. Diamond drop earrings completed the look, and she slid her feet into soft kid-leather stilettos.

Done. Tina caught up a mohair wrap, evening purse, and made her way downstairs.

Nic was waiting in the large entrance foyer, his tall, broad-shouldered frame clothed in a superbly tailored dark suit, white cotton shirt and silk tie.

He looked…incredible. A white-hot sexual animal. All he needed to do to complete the picture was *prowl*.

'Why the faint smile?'

His slight drawl held a tinge of humour, which she matched in response. 'Our first foray into the social jungle.'

'It bothers you?'

It bothers me I'm playing pretend with *you*. With Vasili it had been a game. *Fun.* Nic was a different and totally unpredictable animal.

She walked at his side to the car, slid into the front seat and waited until he gained the street before querying, 'Anything I should know in advance about the people we're visiting?'

'Dimitri and Paul have been friends and business associates for years. Like Stacey, Eleni is Dimitri's second wife. Dimitri has a son from his first marriage, and they have a daughter together. Son married and lives in London; daughter single and lives in New York.' He spared her a quick glance before returning his attention to the road ahead. 'Dimitri and Eleni divide their time between London, New York and Sydney. They flew in from New York last week.'

'Got it.'

What she didn't get was several cars lining the sweeping driveway leading to a magnificent residence high on a hill at Vaucluse.

'I imagined it was dinner for four,' Tina said quietly as Nic slid into a parking bay.

'Dimitri didn't mention anything to the contrary.'

Oh, my. She was being flung in at the deep end. 'Party time.' She sent him a steady look. 'Just spell out the agenda. Am I supposed to appear pensive and quietly secretive? Or shall I gaze at you adoringly?'

'Secretive?'

'As if I'm reflecting on really great sex. Which obviously everyone will imagine we've recently shared.'

'Let's play it by ear, shall we?'

His voice held amusement, and she deliberately widened her eyes.

'Trusting, aren't you?' She opened the passenger door as he slid out from behind the wheel.

'Just remember it takes two.' He crossed to her side and they moved towards the brightly lit entrance.

Within minutes they were shown indoors by an impeccably suited manservant and led into an elegant lounge, announced, and almost immediately enveloped by their host and hostess who greeted them both with affection.

'Tina. Such a pleasure,' Eleni said with a warm smile. 'We have waited a long time for Nic to take a wife.' Friendly, gregarious, she indicated their guests. 'A small gathering of dear friends.' Her features assumed great sadness. 'Vasili...such a tragedy. We were devastated when news reached us.'

'Thank you,' Nic acknowledged, and Tina masked surprise as he placed a casual arm along the back of her waist.

An action that merely projected an expected image, she rationalised as Eleni swept them into the large room. Yet having him so close did strange things to her composure.

Was he aware of it? She fervently hoped not!

Introductions ensued, some of which were unnecessary as Tina was already familiar with a few of the women...some of whom frequently made the social pages of the city's newspapers.

Speculative interest regarding Nic Leandros' new wife was evident. She could sense it, almost *feel* it.

Two uniformed staff offered drinks and hors

d'oeuvres, and she hid her surprise as Nic took two flutes of mineral water and handed her one.

'Solidarity?' Tina queried quietly, and met his warm gaze.

'Of course.'

'Should I thank you?' Her voice held a teasing quality, and her smile resembled warm sunshine.

'I'm sure I'll think of some way.'

'Dinner at the Ritz-Carlton?'

His soft laughter curled round her nerve-ends and tugged a little.

Why *this* man? It didn't make sense. She hardly knew him…his likes and dislikes, his flaws.

'A date?'

She offered a sweet smile. 'Whenever you can fit it into your busy schedule.'

'Nicos!'

A large, jovial, middle-aged man clapped Nic's shoulder while the man's wife drew Tina to one side in what appeared to be a deliberately orchestrated movement.

Divide and conquer?

'Eleni tells me you manage a boutique at Double Bay. My daughter is getting married soon. You must give me the address, and we'll come by.'

'Of course.' She gave the required details with po-lite warmth, recognising the imported designer label the woman was wearing, the Italian handcrafted shoes, the jewellery, the subtle but oh-so-expensive *parfum*.

Tina's trained eye did the maths. Serious money…*very* serious money. Most likely it wasn't

spent locally, but on overseas buying trips and direct
from the designer's Milan salon.

'We must lunch together.'

'Thank you.'

'Vasili...such a tragic end. You knew him, of
course?'

You could say that. 'We were good friends,' Tina
managed quietly, aware the gossip grapevine was
about to go into overdrive.

'So *young.*' There was polite curiosity evident. 'A
little wild, perhaps?'

Fun-loving, believing life was meant to be *lived*,
Vasili had nevertheless possessed a keen mind and
acute business nous.

'I didn't find him so.'

'Nic has the advantage of maturity,' came the con-
fident reply.

And therefore the better choice? She resisted the
urge to gnash her teeth. What was the percentage of
women who consciously chose a man because of his
wealth, maturity, social position?

Yet *she* had. Although *choose* wasn't quite the right
word!

Unbidden, her gaze skimmed the room until it came
to rest on Nic's sculpted features. He was deep in
conversation, and she watched idly for a few seconds,
noting the strength apparent, the well-defined bone
structure. Aware, even from a distance, of his physical
impact, the almost primitive aura he managed to exude without any effort at all.

At that moment he glanced towards her, almost as

if he sensed her light scrutiny, and she saw him say a few words, then move across the room to her side.

'Toula.' His smile held genuine warmth. 'I see you've taken my wife beneath your wing.' He cast Tina a fond look as he reached for her hand and threaded his fingers through her own. 'Darling, there's someone I want you to meet.' He shifted his gaze to the older woman. 'If you'll excuse us?'

Tina barely registered Toula's polite response as she crossed the room at Nic's side.

Darling was definitely overkill. So too was holding her hand so firmly. She tried to pull free, only to have him ease a thumb gently back and forth across the veins at her wrist. An action that momentarily rendered her speechless.

Then she aimed her lacquered nails and dug in, without gaining the slightest reaction. Almost in reflex action he lifted their joined hands and brushed his lips across her knuckles.

Only she could glimpse the expression in those dark eyes, witness the teasing indolence…and something she couldn't define. A vague threat? Or a silent dare?

Well, she could play the game…and play it well. Hadn't she become adept at adopting a façade?

'Careful, *Nicos*.' Her smile was wide, her eyes sparkled, and her voice held a teasing warmth. 'You might be in danger of biting off more than you can chew.'

'Now there's a fascinating thought.' His drawl was pure silk. 'Are you offering a challenge?'

'As long as you're aware it stops the instant we walk out the door.'

It was as well Eleni's manservant drew the guests' attention and announced dinner would be served in the dining-room.

'A reprieve?'

Tina deliberately tilted the edges of her mouth. 'Don't bet on it.'

The dining-room was huge, the table set with fine bone china, cut-crystal goblets, exquisite silverware, with stunning floral decorations placed at precise intervals.

Place-cards indicated seating arrangements, and Tina found herself seated next to an attractive young man whose name she failed to recall.

'Alex,' he enlightened. 'Toula's son.' He waited a beat. 'Formidable, isn't she?'

She didn't pretend to misunderstand. 'Your mother is charming.'

His smile acquired a degree of cynicism. 'Politeness becomes you.'

'A compliment?'

'Of course. If I tell you you're beautiful, will it offend you?'

He was playing with her, teasing in a way that reminded her of Vasili. 'Do you intend offence?'

He looked mildly shocked. 'Of course not.'

She smiled. 'In that case...thank you.'

'You must sample the Chardonnay,' Alex enthused. 'Dimitri has one of the best cellars in Vaucluse.'

'I don't drink.'

His disbelief was barely masked. 'You don't know what you're missing.'

Oh, yes, I do!

Staff began serving the entrée, and she watched Nic fill her goblet with iced water.

'Thanks.'

'You've made a conquest,' he commented quietly.

'Jealous?' It was a light parry that earned her a musing smile.

'Should I be?'

The edge of her mouth twitched a little. 'I guess a new husband might be proprietorial.'

Nic forked a morsel from his plate and fed it to her, giving her little option but to part her lips and accept the food.

'Thank you, darling.'

'My pleasure.'

He was good, so good even she could almost believe he meant it. Except it was just a game…one she could play equally well. As she had done with Vasili. They'd even had a name for it…*flirting mode*.

So what's the difference? she queried silently.

Except Vasili had been both friend and confidant. As familiar as a brother she could trust. She'd known his mind, his thoughts, almost as well as she knew her own.

Nic, on the other hand, was an enigma. Instinct warned there was much beneath the surface…like an iceberg. Although *ice* in its true interpretation didn't apply. The man was hot, effortlessly projecting a sensual heat that had a devastating effect on the opposite sex.

Apart from his physical attributes, there was something about his eyes—their depth—almost as if he had seen much and *knew* the intricacies of the human mind. A rare and special quality coveted by many and possessed by few.

And as a lover? She had the instinctive feeling he knew it all. Where to touch to drive a woman wild beyond reason…and catch her as she fell.

Wasn't that how lovemaking was supposed to be? Two people so in tune with each other that what they shared together was uniquely *theirs*.

Indulging in thought-provoking reflection at a dinner table filled with a complement of guests wasn't conducive to clarity of mind.

'My dear, you must tell us where Nic intends taking you for the honeymoon.'

The words were accompanied by a light feminine laugh, and Tina offered a faint smile. 'It's difficult to get away right now.'

'Of course. But soon, surely?'

Tina turned towards Nic. 'The Greek Islands would be nice, darling.'

His eyes met her sparkling gaze. 'You must allow me to surprise you.'

'How lovely.' Her voice was almost a feline purr, and she managed to keep her expression intact as he smiled and brushed light fingers across her cheek.

The soft pink suddenly colouring her features was uncontrived, and she concentrated on finishing the last morsel of food as staff began collecting plates prior to serving the next course.

One of several, each served with a different wine. Talk was convivial and it seemed hours before Dimitri suggested they adjourn to the lounge for coffee.

'Tired?'

Tina met Nic's dark gaze with equanimity. 'A little.'

'We'll leave soon.'

He managed their departure with ease, and within minutes the Lexus was traversing the arterial road down towards Rose Bay.

'You managed to charm everyone,' Nic drawled as they entered the house.

She sent him a measured look as he reset the security system. 'Should I thank you for doing likewise?'

They gained the curved staircase and ascended it together.

'I imagine you've gained a few new clients.'

'You think? Friends tend to want a higher than usual discount.' There was an edge of cynicism apparent, and she tempered it with a slight smile. 'I have a firm discount policy. No exceptions.'

He wouldn't mind observing her in action... managerial youth versus cashed-up matrons well versed in driving a hard bargain.

They reached the upper floor and Tina turned towards the wing where her suite lay. 'Goodnight.'

'You forgot something.'

She gave him a puzzled look. 'What?'

'This.' He leant in and fastened his mouth over hers in a brief, evocative kiss that tore her composure to shreds.

His eyes speared hers, their expression unfathomable. 'Sleep well.'

Then he moved towards the opposite wing without so much as a backward glance.

Tina stood immobile for several long seconds. *What was that?*

A salutatory gesture?

Sure, and piglets fly!

Attempting to analyse his agenda...if indeed he had one...occupied her mind until sleep provided a welcome release.

CHAPTER FIVE

'OH, wow,' Lily voiced quietly. 'What I wouldn't give to look like that.'

Tina glanced up from checking an invoice and saw a stunningly beautiful young woman move into the salon. Tall, waist-length sable hair, incredible facial features, exquisite make-up, and attired in avant-garde couture very few women could get away with.

Sultry, Tina accorded. Of the jungle feline variety. A woman who could devour a man, then spit out the pieces.

Wow didn't come close.

'Yours or mine?'

'Oh, please,' Tina declared *sotto voce*. 'Be my guest.'

Lily was the consummate fashion consultant, possessed of an incredible knowledge of fabric, design, local and international designers. She also had a flair for putting things together, how the positioning of a silk scarf could turn a beautifully crafted garment into something spectacular.

Tina was aware of the young woman's voice, the rather haughty air and the faint sting of criticism as she examined and discarded one garment after another.

She gave Lily another five minutes before going into rescue mode.

'Is there anything I can help you with?'

Up close the woman's beauty was even more stunning, for her skin was flawless beneath skilfully applied cosmetics, and her hair… It was like a river of sable flowing loose down her back, shifting like satin with every movement.

'The list of designers embracing your window cites you stock Giorgio Armani.'

Tina knew Lily would have shown what stock they had. 'We carry a limited seasonal range.' She indicated the appropriate rack. 'This is what we have to offer for summer.'

She received a cool sweeping glance. 'Presumably your salon cannot afford to offer a comprehensive selection?'

Tina ignored the urge to rise to the bait. 'We cater exclusively to our existing clientele base and aim to be appropriate to the Sydney social scene.'

'Hmm,' the beautiful one dismissed. 'This—' she indicated the rack with a dismissive gesture '—is hopeless. I shall have to wait until I'm in Paris next month.'

'You have that option.'

An elegant hand indicated three pairs of stiletto shoes with matching bags displayed at intervals along one wall. 'Are these all you have?'

Difficult, *picky*…and, Tina suspected, filling in time before meeting a friend for lunch.

'They're merely suggestions, and, if you check the printed card, available in the exclusive shoe boutique in the arcade adjacent the Ritz-Carlton hotel.'

'I expect personalised service.'

Okay, so this was going to be a doozey. Time to sugar-coat business facts. 'Should you purchase an outfit, Lily will only be too pleased to help you with any further selections within the immediate area.'

Cool dark eyes swept Tina's frame, resting momentarily on her hair. 'You would do well to add highlights and wear your hair loose.'

'It's my day for the upswept look,' she responded without missing a beat, and received a pitying glance in return.

With a scornful, dismissive gaze, the woman turned and walked…*glided*, to the door and exited the boutique.

'*Well.*' Lily's voice was a long drawn-out descriptive that said it all.

'Oh, yeah, in spades.'

The rest of the day settled into a customary routine, with a phone call from Nic relaying he'd be home late.

The thought of returning to a large, empty house didn't hold much appeal.

'Feel like taking in a movie?' It was a spur-of-the-moment suggestion, and caught Lily's interest.

'DVD or the cinema?'

'Big screen,' Tina elaborated. 'Dinner first?'

'You're on. What time and where?'

She named a café, gave a time, and sent Nic an SMS message when she raced home to exchange her elegant suit for dress-jeans, tee shirt and jacket.

Pizza washed down with a cold drink satisfied them perfectly, and the movie was pure escapist fun from which they emerged relaxed and light-hearted.

'Want to go somewhere for coffee?'

Lily arched an eyebrow. 'No rush to get home to your hunk of a husband?'

At that moment her cellphone pealed, and she picked up to discover Nic on the line.

'I'm leaving the city now.'

The advance call, Tina realised. 'Lily and I are stopping off for coffee.'

'Tell me where, and I'll join you.'

She looked at Lily and mouthed, *Where?* Heard her friend's response, and relayed the venue.

'Be there in ten.'

The café was within a short walking distance, and well patronised. Finding a table involved being exceedingly quick the instant one became empty, which they managed, and no sooner had they given their order than two young men asked if they could share.

'Sorry, there's someone joining us,' Lily refused, only to have them pull out two chairs and sit down.

'They're not here yet.'

Tina looked from one to the other. 'If that's a pick-up line, it needs work.'

'Maybe you could help me improve on it.'

It was difficult not to laugh at his overt suggestive tone. 'Why don't you go practise on someone else?'

'An excellent idea,' a familiar voice drawled silkily, and she turned to see Nic standing immediately behind, his expression polite, although only a fool would ignore the silent threat lurking in those dark eyes.

He rested a hand on her shoulder and lowered his

head to brush his lips to her temple. 'Problems, darling?'

'Nothing Lily and I can't handle.' Sensation feathered the length of her spine, and she inwardly cursed her own vulnerability.

It's merely an *act*, nothing more. For the love of heaven, she didn't want it to be *real*...did she? To tread that path would lead to a madness she could ill afford.

In the guise of deception she gifted Nic a warm smile, and watched with interest as the two young men wilted beneath Nic's steady gaze and promptly vacated the table.

'Lily,' Nic acknowledged as he slid into the seat at Tina's side and ordered coffee from the hovering waitress.

Afterwards Tina had little recollection of their conversation, except that it touched lightly on the movie they'd just seen and Lily's amusing anecdote regarding the day's difficult client.

'He's to die for,' Lily said softly as she brushed her cheek to Tina's when they parted. 'See you tomorrow.' She turned towards Nic. 'Thanks for coffee.'

'My pleasure.'

Tina stood at Nic's side as Lily slid into her car, and Tina lifted a hand in farewell.

'Where are you parked?'

She told him, and they walked half a block to where her bright yellow Volkswagen stood beneath a streetlight.

'I'm on the next corner,' Nic informed her as she unlocked the door. 'Wait and I'll follow you.'

'Why?'

'Just do it, Tina.'

Her chin tilted. 'You're being ridiculous.'

He touched a thumb to the centre of her mouth. 'Wait.' Without a further word he turned and walked with fluid ease towards the corner.

She slid in behind the wheel, ignited the engine and headed towards Rose Bay, uncaring of his reaction. For years she'd driven home alone. Why should now be any different?

A steady flow of traffic occupied the main arterial road, and she refrained from checking her rear-vision mirror until she reached the gated entrance leading to Nic's home.

Impossible to imagine he wouldn't have caught up with her, and she wasn't surprised to see his car slide into the garage beside her own.

Two engines died simultaneously, closely followed by the closing of two car doors as the garage doors automatically whirred shut.

'Wilful defiance, or determination to oppose me?' His tone was deceptively quiet and too controlled.

Tina met his steady gaze with unflinching disregard. 'Why not both?'

The atmosphere suddenly became highly charged… electric…as she fought a silent battle for supremacy.

'Let's go inside, shall we?'

She lifted her shoulders in a careless gesture. 'The garage has a certain…ambience, don't you think?'

'You want to walk, or be carried?'

The silky tones sent a sudden shiver down her spine. 'You might drop me.' Facetiousness was one way of dealing with the situation.

Was that a quick gleam of humour in those dark eyes...or a figment of her imagination?

'I managed perfectly last time.'

Nevertheless she preceded him to the house and entered the foyer. 'Where do you want to hold the inquisition?'

'The kitchen?'

'Ah...informality,' Tina quipped. 'It could have meant serious trouble if you'd suggested your study.'

Minutes later she turned to face him in the large, modern, well-equipped kitchen. 'Do I get to have a glass of water before or after the lecture?'

The edge of his mouth twisted a little. 'I need you to identify a woman from a clipping in last month's Melbourne newspaper.'

He was serious, she perceived. 'You think I might know her?'

'It's possible you may already have met.'

'And you've deduced this...how?'

'From Lily's description of your difficult customer.'

Oh, boy. 'The drop-dead gorgeous person with waist-length dark hair?'

'The same.'

'She has a name?'

He pushed a hand into his trouser pocket. 'Sabine Lafarge.'

'A lover?' There was nothing she could do about

the painful sinking feeling deep within. 'Past or present?'

His eyes met and held hers. 'Past.'

'And you're telling me this…because?'

'I ended the relationship months ago.'

'She doesn't want to let go?'

'No.'

How was it possible for one small word to hold such a wealth of meaning? 'She's obsessed with you.' It was a statement rather than a query. It was hard to inject humour into her tone as she tilted her head. 'Must be your charm, wealth and sexual prowess.' She even managed a faint smile. 'My bet is on the last two…in that order.'

'This from someone who has no knowledge of the latter?'

She didn't allow her eyes to wander from his. 'For which I'm eternally grateful.' She told herself it was the truth. The emotional disturbances of late were re-lated to pregnancy hormones.

'Go show me the news-clipping.'

'It's in a file in the study.'

He had a *file* on the woman?

Minutes later she watched as he unlocked a filing cabinet, extracted a slim folder and lay it open on the large executive desk.

There, captured on photographic celluloid, was the woman who'd visited the boutique. The pose in the shot was practised, the facial features perfectly aligned, the eyes wide and luminous. She bore the confidence of a woman who had everything…and knew it.

'Yes,' Tina said simply. 'Is she likely to be a problem?'

Nic closed the file and replaced it in the cabinet. 'I sought legal counsel. Stalking,' he elaborated as he turned to face her. 'Hence the file.'

'And now you think she's intent on targeting me?'

A muscle bunched at the edge of his jaw. 'It looks that way.' He waited a beat. 'As from tomorrow a live-in bodyguard will occupy the self-contained living quarters over the garages. Ostensibly his presence will be perceived as butler and household help.'

'Isn't that overkill?'

'I'll curtail travelling interstate and overseas to a minimum.'

'What on earth do you think she's going to do? *Attack* me?'

His eyes hardened. 'She has a perfidious *modus operandi*. I won't have you exposed to it.'

Well, *really*. 'I'm capable of defending myself.' Lessons learned, she admitted silently.

He reached out a hand and trailed light fingers down her cheek. 'I'm not prepared to take the chance.'

Because of the child she carried.

A wild thought raced through her head…what if she miscarried?

Cold, hard fact provided an answer. Nic would end the marriage.

Then she could go back to living the life she'd led before Nic Leandros turned *life*, as she knew it, upside down.

A degree of anger rose to the surface at his obdurate

stand. 'What if I don't *want* someone shadowing my every move?'

'Tough,' he stated with a finality that sent shivers feathering down her spine.

She glared at him. 'Right now, I don't like you very much.'

'I guess I can live with it.'

Tina picked up the closest object to hand—a crystal paperweight—and threw it at him, watching in detached fascination as he fielded it easily and carefully replaced it out of her reach.

Then he looked at her, and she almost died at the silent threat in those dark eyes. 'Go,' he bade in a dangerously soft voice. 'Before I do something regrettable.'

She wouldn't run. Instead she raked her eyes over his tall frame from head to toe and back again, then turned and walked from the room, shoulders squared, her head held high.

It wasn't until she reached her bedroom suite and closed the door behind her that she permitted herself to reflect on what had just happened. She sank back against the door.

She had to be insane to try to best him. Mad to think she *could*.

CHAPTER SIX

SATURDAY was one of the busiest trading days of the week, and the day didn't disappoint as clients visited to check out new season's stock.

Spring was evident in early blooms: trees that had lain bare during winter were sprouting new growth, and the sun's warmth fingered the earth, bringing promise of a mild summer.

There was no sign of Sabine, for which Tina was grateful. Although she considered it unlikely the woman would appear again so soon.

Two guests who attended Eleni and Dimitri's dinner called in to browse. Toula, Tina recalled, who, after much deliberation and consultation with her friend, finally reached a decision to purchase the expensive ensemble.

'You arrange a discount for me?'

The haggling was about to begin. Tina offered the customary percentage, and saw Toula's eyebrows lift.

'But we are friends. Thirty per cent.'

Friends? I've met you *once*. 'This item is new season stock,' she explained. 'Not a sale item.'

'But you would discount at least twenty per cent if it were.'

'If the garment is still in stock by January, you would be welcome to twenty per cent,' Tina managed evenly.

'So we consider it is January and you give it to me less thirty per cent. Twenty per cent sale and ten per cent for a friend.'

With a light laugh and a teasing shake of her head Tina collected the garment from the counter and began transferring it onto the clothes hanger. 'You're good at this, Toula.' But not good enough. 'My original discount stands.'

'But that's outrageous!' Toula leaned in close. 'I can bring you plenty of business.'

Time for the hard word, politely couched. 'I manage the boutique on behalf of the owner,' she said quietly. 'It is she who sets the percentage scale.'

'I will go elsewhere.'

'As you wish. However the garment you've chosen is a designer original, for which this boutique has exclusivity.'

Toula's lips pursed. 'I shall think about it.'

'Would you like me to put it aside for an hour?' She checked her watch, then proffered a gracious smile. 'If you're not here by three, I'll return it to stock.'

'Very well.'

'She'll be back,' Lily declared when the two women exited the shop.

'Maybe.'

'She loved the garment, she looks good in it, she has money…ergo, she'll buy it.' Lily's grin had an impish quality. 'Latte on me after work if I'm wrong.'

'Done.'

Toula swept into the boutique at precisely one minute to three and handed over her credit card. 'You drive a hard bargain.'

Was it Tina's imagination, or did she detect a measure of respect? 'I run a successful business,' she corrected gently. 'I'm sure you have the right shoes and bag,' she added, drawing Toula's attention to the items on display. 'But these are splendid, don't you think?'

Toula inspected both and made a snap decision. 'If you can organise the shoes in my size, I'll take them.'

'Allow me to phone and check.'

Five minutes later she'd made a commission on the sale, Toula was a satisfied client, and Tina owed Lily a latte.

It was almost five when they shut down the boutique, and within minutes they were sharing a table at a nearby café with two decaf lattes on order.

'Nothing planned for the evening?'

How could she admit she had no idea? 'A quiet meal at home.' That should cover it.

Lily wriggled her eyebrows and her eyes acquired a teasing gleam. 'A little wine, fine food…and an early night?'

'Uh-huh.' It was a sufficiently noncommittal response.

'Sunday tomorrow,' Lily ventured with an impish grin. 'You can stay in bed and enjoy each other.' A wistful sigh whispered through her lips and her eyes acquired a dreamy quality. 'I bet he's just fabulous.'

Probably, but let's not go there.

What if she were to confide the marriage didn't

involve sex? Worse, that she was pregnant with Nic's brother's child?

Tina Matheson, well educated with strict moral values, *friend*...was paying big time for one foolish mistake.

Yet there were those who'd argue, given Nic's rugged attractiveness, wealth and social status...*what's your problem*?

Because it's not who I am, nor who I want to be.

A complex answer that wasn't any answer at all.

A waitress delivered two lattes, and Tina sipped the steaming milky brew with appreciation.

'Nothing to say?' Lily quizzed, and Tina summoned a faint smile.

'There are some things which should remain private.'

'Oh, damn,' Lily denounced good-naturedly. 'Just when I thought the conversation was going to get interesting.'

'Let's focus on *you* for a change, huh?'

'One word encapsulates it all. *Waiting*. For the right man, the right life, all my dreams fulfilled. I keep looking, and there's no one out there. At least, no one who wants to commit.'

'Maybe you're looking in all the wrong places.'

Lily leaned forward. 'I want the shooting stars, clashes of cymbals...all that to-die-for stuff. Maybe I'm just going to have to settle for *comfortable*.'

'And that would be so bad?' Tina teased.

'Easy for you to say when you have Mr Gorgeous.'

A cellphone pealed, Tina checked her own and when she picked up Nic was on the line.

'About done for the day?' Video digital ensured she could glimpse a lazy smile broadening his generous masculine mouth.

She panned the cellphone towards Lily. 'Grabbing a latte and some down time after a busy day.'

'SMS me when you leave.'

'See you soon. Bye.' And closed the connection.

'The main man?'

'How did you guess?'

Lily grinned. 'Calling you home, huh?'

Playing check-in Charlie, she corrected silently. 'Reminding me I'm no longer a single woman.'

Lily rolled her eyes. 'As if you'd forget!'

Enough already. Tina extracted a note to cover the bill, and rose to her feet. 'Let's go, shall we?'

Dusk was falling as they walked to their respective cars parked alongside each other in a staff bay. 'Have a great weekend,' she bade fondly as Lily unlocked her vehicle. 'See you Monday.'

The Volkswagen's engine ignited like a charm, and Tina headed towards the arterial road leading to Rose Bay.

The traffic lights were against her as she paused at a major intersection, and an inexplicable prickling sensation crawled over both shoulders and centred at the base of her neck.

Weird, definitely weird. It was Saturday evening, for heaven's sake, there were cars in every direction.

Yet the prickling sensation remained despite an effort to dismiss it.

Auto-suggestion, she rationalised as she activated the mechanism releasing the front gates. There wasn't anyone following her...hadn't she checked her rear-vision mirror several times since turning into Rose Bay?

Tina garaged the car and entered the house. A shower, change of clothes, and something to eat would be good.

She moved towards the stairs, only to come to an abrupt halt as Nic descended from the upper level.

Jeans and a dark polo shirt gave him a whole different look. One that warranted a second glance. His breadth of shoulder was impressive, so too was the tight musculature of his upper torso, the bunched biceps.

'Hi.' The greeting sounded inane as they met midway.

'Tough day?'

She met his gaze with equanimity. 'Just busy.'

'Steve has prepared dinner.'

'The bodyguard *cooks*?'

'Weekends,' Nic relayed. 'If we decide to eat in.'

'Just one of his many talents?'

'Why not ask him?'

Tina's eyes flared wide. 'He's not in the kitchen?'

'Right behind you, ma'am.'

The *ma'am* did it. Tall, muscle-bound, young...and Texan, Tina surmised as she turned to face him.

How wrong could you be? The man who stood facing her was of average height, possessed of a lean, wiry build, nondescript and in his mid-forties.

'Not what you expected?'

'Please tell me I got the Texan bit right?'

Blue eyes crinkled with humour. 'Dallas born and bred.'

'Thank heavens.'

Steve shot Nic a musing glance. 'I think we're going to get along just fine.'

'Next, you'll tell me you're old friends.'

'We go back a while,' Nic revealed, and she lifted a hand and trailed fingers along his jaw-line.

'More obsessive women among the skeletons in your closet, darling?'

He caught her hand, brushed his lips to the centre of her palm…and watched her eyes flare with shocked surprise. And an emotion she was quick to hide.

'Why don't you go change?' he queried evenly. 'Dinner will be in half an hour. Afterwards Steve will take a run-through with you.'

Tina retrieved her hand and eyeballed both men. 'I kick-box and have a black belt in karate.'

'A definite advantage,' Steve conceded with a lazy grin.

There was dignity in retreat, and she managed it with ease, only to hear Nic's voice as she reached the upper level. 'I'll be there in a few minutes.'

'To scrub my back?' The words slipped out before she gave them thought.

'You have only to ask.'

As if.

Warm colour tinged her cheeks at his drawled response, and she silently cursed her wayward tongue.

Twenty minutes later she'd showered and changed into dress-jeans and a soft cotton top. Her hair was a slightly damp mass of curls, which she swept into a knot atop her head and secured with a series of broad clips.

A tantalising aroma teased the air as she neared the kitchen, and she entered on impulse to see Nic leaning a hip against a bench-top nursing a glass of wine while Steve spooned what appeared to be a succulent beef stew into a serving dish.

'That smells great. Need any help?'

Steve indicated a dish of assorted vegetables. 'You can take that through to the dining-room. Nic and I will bring the rest.'

It soon became apparent the two men were friends rather than employer and employee, and their exchange of several anecdotes during the meal made for a relaxed, convivial atmosphere.

If Steve's aim was to put her at ease, he succeeded, Tina admitted silently. Although as much couldn't be said for Nic, whose mere presence was sufficient to set her nerves jangling in self-protective mode.

Why *was* that? She couldn't be attracted to him, surely? At least not in any sexual sense. Yet pheromones were working a subtle magic, tugging at her sensual heart and causing havoc of a kind she could well do without.

Just the look of him did it for her. The way he moved, his strong profile, the tiny lines fanning from his eyes and the sensual curve of his mouth.

She had instant recall of how it felt, the fleeting touch, the brief slide of his tongue over her own.

There was a part of her, buried deep inside, that wanted more, much more. The touch of his hands on her body, cupping each curve, exploring each indentation…bringing her *alive*.

Except such thoughts were the stuff of dreams; reality was a bad memory and issues of trust.

The stew was delicious, and so too was the apple crumble dessert. She gave Steve the compliment he deserved.

Tina declined coffee and settled for tea, then she insisted on clearing up, despite Steve's protestations.

As it was, the three of them made short work of kitchen duties before retreating to Nic's study where the scene became strictly business.

'We need to set down a few fail-safe rules,' Steve outlined as soon as they were comfortably settled in three leather chairs. 'No exceptions.'

'Don't you think all this is over-the-top?'

'We're not dealing with a rational person. Sabine's psychotic delusions lead her to believe the unbelievable, and she'll do almost anything to gain her objective.' Steve's gaze became inflexible. 'To date, Sabine has already broken an existing Restraining Order in Melbourne. Nic's recent move to Sydney and his marriage have merely escalated the situation. She has already relocated here.'

'So, what do you propose?'

'I want you to carry an electronic tracking device. One in your car, one on your person.'

Tina closed her eyes and opened them again. 'You have to be kidding?'

Steve didn't answer. 'You check in when you arrive at the boutique each morning, and check out when you leave at the end of each day.'

She couldn't help herself. 'Next you'll tell me we're to share a secret code.'

'That, too. Linked to me, Nic and a private security firm.'

Tina looked from one to the other. 'I'm not buying into this.'

'It's not negotiable,' Nic stated with chilling softness.

'The child I carry is so important?'

'Mother and child.'

Of course, for without the mother there is no child.

If she didn't get out of here, she'd say something reprehensible. Plus there was dignity in silence. It didn't stop the resentment…*rage*, she amended as she rose to her feet and walked to the door, paused, then turned to direct Nic a searing glare.

To hell with dignity. 'I hate you.'

The temptation to slam the door behind her was almost irresistible, except she showed great restraint and pulled it closed with an almost silent click.

Dear heaven. She needed to feel fresh air on her face and walk off some of her anger.

Dammit, there was so much of it. Aimed at herself, Vasili, *Nic*. Not to mention the intruder whose actions caused such emotional damage.

Damage she'd thought she'd dealt with. And she *had*, she reassured herself silently as she unlocked the front door and stepped out into the night.

She didn't need a therapist to confirm that she was fighting a mental battle with her emotional heart. One she'd buried deep beneath so many protective layers;

the dispensing of each was proving the cause of her self-anguish and pain.

The day will arrive when you'll discover love and need to conquer the last barrier.

To which she'd responded *Feel the fear, and do it anyway?*

You'll need to let go.

At the time, and in the years since, she was convinced she'd never allow herself to become emotionally involved. It was all about control, and she'd learned the lesson well by playing safe. Until one unguarded moment had resulted in the unforeseeable.

Now she was thrust into a situation she didn't want, and some fickle imp was intent on turning her life upside down.

Tina hugged her arms close over her chest as she walked the perimeter of the grounds. There was a moon high in the dark velvet sky, casting sufficient light for her to see where she stepped. The large wrought-iron gates guarding the property were closed and electronically locked. Not that it mattered, for she had no intention of venturing out onto the street.

Physical attraction wasn't love, not even close, she rationalised as she trod dew-damp grass. Heavens, she didn't even *like* Nic.

He was everything she disliked in a man. Ruthless, powerful, *relentless*. Sensitivity? She doubted he had one sensitive bone in his body.

She made a second turn around the perimeter, uncaring of the cool evening air. After the fourth turn she retraced her steps to the front entrance and re-entered the house.

Nic stood leaning indolently against the balustrade at the base of the staircase, his expression inscrutable as she drew close.

'Are you done?'

Tina lifted her chin and threw him a look that would have felled a lesser man. 'It was either a walk in fresh air, or do you an injury.' She drew herself up to her full height and glared at him. 'And if you dare suggest I take myself off to bed, I'll hit you.'

'I was about to recommend a hot drink.'

She derived immense satisfaction from telling him exactly what he could do with his recommendation, then she moved past him and ascended the stairs.

The fact she went to her suite, undressed and slid into bed had nothing to do with it, because *she* made the decision.

CHAPTER SEVEN

IT BEGAN as it always did…Tina was in a darkened bedroom, night, asleep and dreamless. Then the sound, so soft it barely lifted her from the subconscious.

It came again, a slight swishing noise as if someone or something brushed against the drapes at the sliding door leading onto her small apartment balcony.

She opened one eye, fractionally, caught a faint movement, and knew in that frightening second she was no longer alone in the room.

Her heartbeat went into overdrive as fear raced through her body. Surely he must hear it. She could.

Close your eyes, breathe evenly. He'll think you're asleep. Isn't that what the police advised…don't confront?

The silence ate at her. Where was he? Apart from heavy movable objects, anything of value was in her room.

Each second seemed like an hour, yet still she couldn't detect the slightest sound.

He was close. She could sense him, smell the odour of cigarette smoke…and something else. Body sweat.

Please, *please*, she silently begged. Just take what you want and go.

There was a whisper of sound as he slid open the

drawer of her bedside pedestal, the faint rustle as he removed her jewellery box and emptied the contents.

Go, she urged. *Go.*

The next instant the covers were torn from the bed, and she cried out as hard hands caught hold of her body, holding her down.

Dear God, *no.* It was a silent scream that didn't find voice.

Then she did scream as he gripped the hem of her nightshirt and dragged it over her face, pinning it there as he sank his teeth into her breast.

She fought like a demon, kicking out, flailing her fists anywhere she could connect, and she cried out as he captured one, then the other and wrenched them high above her head.

Bitch. The word was a guttural snarl as he rose above her.

Instinct, self-survival, was responsible for the desperate knee she dug into his groin. The mixture of elation and fear as it connected, his grunt of pain, her release as he rolled onto the floor.

Escape was uppermost in her mind. Out of the room, the apartment. *Go.*

'Tina.' Hands were on her shoulders, and she fought like a wildcat.

'For the love of God. Come out of it.'

Still she fought, so caught up in the nightmare it had become reality.

Except it began to change, shifting to a scenario she was unfamiliar with. She knew what followed...and it wasn't *this.*

The intruder in her nightmare didn't carry her. Nor did he call her by name. What...

She opened her eyes, only to close them momentarily as realisation hit. It was no longer dark. She wasn't in her apartment or a hotel room. She was in Nic Leandros' home. It all came flooding back, and with it...relief. Relief that was short-lived when she saw she wasn't in her suite...but *his*. What was more her nightshirt was riding high beyond decency. And Nic didn't appear to be wearing anything except a towel hitched at his waist.

'How often do you get these nightmares?'

Dammit, he could still hear her screams. The first one had shaken him to the core as he'd hit the floor running, and he'd witnessed the second, seen the fear, the shock etching her pale features. Her eyes. As long as he lived, he'd never forget the expression etched in those beautiful green depths, or how dark they'd become.

'Put me down.'

Not yet.

'Please.'

The *please* did it. Except he merely let her slide to her feet and he curved his hands over her shoulders.

'I'm fine. I'll go back to my room now.'

She was far from fine. What was more, he didn't want her tucked away in a suite on the opposite side of the house, any more than he wanted to be jolted out of sleep by her distant screams.

'Do you want to talk about that night?'

Nic watched her eyelids flutter down, then sweep upwards. 'I was all talked out years ago.'

'Yet the nightmares still persist.'

A shiver ran over the surface of her skin. 'Occasionally.'

'You're cold.' Without a word he slid his hands down her back and pulled her in, all too aware how she fitted against him.

He sensed the clean, fresh smell of her hair, the faint lingering touch of her perfume, and pressed his chin to her forehead.

For a few seconds she stood absolutely still, almost afraid to move. He felt so...good. Being held by him, the slight muskiness of his skin against her cheek, the gentleness beneath the hard musculature.

She had the strangest desire to sink in against him, to lift her hands and clasp them at his nape, then pull his head down to hers.

Except such an action was tantamount to madness.

'I want you close. Where I can see you...hear you in the night.' He felt her stiffen, and he released her, stepping back a pace. He leant down and tossed back the covers on the bed. 'Tonight you sleep here.'

Tina looked at him, and almost wished she hadn't, for there was too much smooth skin stretched over muscle and sinew. He was altogether *too much*. The powerful shoulders, washboard stomach, too *male* for any woman's peace of mind...much less hers.

Share a bed with him? Was he insane?

'Sleeping with you isn't part of the deal.'

His dark eyes held hers. 'The operative word is *sleep*.'

Her chin tilted a little. 'You expect me to trust you?'

'You have my word.'

She'd lived alone for years, with no one there to hold, comfort, help soothe a vivid memory as it returned to haunt her.

'I'd prefer to go back to my room.' She moved away from him and nearly died when he turned her round to face him. Stark fear chased across her expressive features for an instant, then it was masked.

His husky oath sounded vicious.

'For the love of heaven.' He swept an arm beneath her knees and slid onto the large bed with her, caught up the covers, curved her body in against his own and anchored her there.

'Relax.'

Please. As if that were going to happen any time soon.

If she were to struggle, what would he do?

'Don't go there.'

He read minds?

'Mistake me for someone else through the night, and I won't be responsible for my reaction,' Tina vowed quietly.

'Go to sleep.'

She silently damned him to hell.

Minutes later she felt his breathing settle into a deep, rhythmic pattern, and she waited, counting the minutes until she felt it was safe to inch her way slowly from the bed.

At least, that was the plan. Except it didn't happen, for each time she made a surreptitious move, his arm tightened.

He was asleep…she was sure of it. That deep, steady breathing couldn't be faked. Or could it?

There was something incredibly comforting about being held like this. The human warmth, security…feeling *safe*. It was nice.

Oh, for goodness' sake, she mentally derided. *Get real.* She'd never been so aware of a man in her life!

There was little she could do to control the wild images racing through her head. How would it feel to have his lips brush her nape and seek the vulnerable hollow at the edge of her neck? Turn her in his arms and trail a path to her breasts and linger there, savour each tender peak before tracing a line to her waist, and edge lower to taste, caress.

Then ease inside her…would he fit?

Enough! *Get a grip.*

What was the matter with her? This *feeling*…it was just chemistry. Nothing to do with the man himself.

She had every reason to hate the way he'd intruded, threatened, and taken over her life. And she did hate him for what he'd done. So, too, for what he was about to expose her to with Sabine.

To remain here, quiescent, was impossible. Five minutes, and she'd give easing out from his arms another try.

That was the last thing she remembered, and when she woke it was morning, an early silvery light filtered into the room…and she was alone in the large bed.

There was no *ohmigod* moment. She remembered with vivid clarity the nightmare and its aftermath. Just as she recalled falling asleep in Nic's arms.

However, it wasn't going to happen again.

With resolve she slid from beneath the covers, returned to her suite, showered, dressed in jeans and top, and went down to the kitchen to get something to eat.

Of Nic there was no sign, for which she told herself she was grateful. Steve sat out on the terrace drinking coffee, and she lifted a hand in greeting.

He rose to his feet and entered the kitchen. 'I'll make you breakfast.'

'Please,' Tina protested. 'I can fix it myself.'

'Nic asked me to tell you he took the early flight to Melbourne. He'll be back tonight.'

The prospect of a carefree day held definite appeal, and her heart felt lighter as she gathered fruit and yoghurt, popped toast and made tea.

'Do you have any plans?'

She read him in an instant. 'Like going out beyond the locked gates?' An expressive eye-roll said it all. 'Maybe, in a few hours.' First she had some data to check on the laptop, then she'd call her mother. After that, the day was hers. 'Do I need permission?'

Her frivolous query was met with Steve's steady gaze.

'I've already fitted a tracking device to your car. There are just a few things I need to explain, then you're clear to go.'

Tina lifted both hands and mimicked quotation marks. 'The secret code.'

'I suggest you treat this seriously.'

'Got it.' She carried her breakfast to the table.

He took on a stern, almost military persona. 'Do you think Nic would put me here at considerable expense on a nebulous whim?'

She had to agree, and admitted reluctantly, 'I guess not.'

'So.' He drew the word out. 'Remain alert. Don't be a hero.' He paused for a few telling seconds. 'And report the slightest incident. Even if you think it's irrelevant.'

She reflected on the goose-bumps while driving home from work... No, it was nothing.

'Spell it out.'

'What is it with you and Nic? You read minds?'

'Faces,' Steve enlightened.

'And mine is particularly transparent?'

'Unguarded.'

And she thought she was doing so well! 'It was just a feeling,' she offered slowly as his eyes sharpened.

'Never ignore an instinct. You didn't see anything untoward? A car following you into this street?'

Tina shook her head. 'No. I checked.'

'We'll talk when you've had breakfast.'

She took time to update data into her laptop, rang her mother for their usual Sunday morning chat, then she grabbed a jacket, bag, caught up her keys and went in search of Steve.

There was effectiveness in simplicity, and, mindful of his caution, she set off for Darling Harbour where she browsed for a while, bought a pair of earrings that caught her eye, picked up a falafel and bottled water and demolished both as she wandered through the maze of lower-level shops.

It was almost five when she headed towards Rose Bay, and on impulse she stopped by her apartment, saw the painting was finished, the tiling completed, and the new carpet had been fitted. There was only the electrician to connect new kitchen white goods, install new light fixtures, then she could move her furniture in from storage.

The question rose to mind as to whether she should keep the apartment empty or lease it out.

She shook her head at the prospect of it being tenanted when she'd gone to considerable expense to refurbish.

Decisions, she reflected as she returned to her car. Something caught her eye as she unlocked the door. Paper, undoubtedly a flier, was tucked beneath a windscreen wiper, and she removed and tossed it onto the passenger seat to dispose of later.

Nic's Lexus was in the garage when she reached home, and she ran lightly upstairs to change before joining the men for dinner.

Tailored trousers and a loose light woollen top, she decided. Five minutes to freshen up, and she'd be done in ten.

Or would have, except when she opened the walk-in robe it was empty. What...? She crossed to the chest of drawers and pulled out one, then the others...all empty.

Where?

'I've moved it all down to my suite.'

Tina turned slowly to face the owner of that drawling voice and saw Nic leaning against the door-jamb, casually dressed in jeans and thin woollen jumper that moulded his muscular frame to perfection.

Calm, she should remain calm, she admonished silently.

'Why did you do that?'

'Because that's where you'll be sleeping from now on.'

He watched as those green eyes acquired a fiery tinge. They mirrored her every mood, and right now there was no question as to her anger.

'You can just move them back again,' she managed tightly. 'Or, better yet, I will.'

'By all means.' He straightened and stood to one side as she brushed past him. 'Just be sure I'll move them back again.'

She flung him a stormy look. 'Then we're both going to be busy.'

'It would seem so.'

Of all the dictatorial, pitiless men, Tina fumed as she entered the master suite…and came to an abrupt halt at the sight of Nic's large bed moved off centre to accommodate another bed, not quite as wide, but close.

Clearly intended for *her*.

Well, he could think again. No way was she sharing his suite.

She crossed to the nearest walk-in robe, swore briefly beneath her breath when she discovered it was *his*, and crossed to the other, gathered up everything on hangers and carried them to the opposite wing of the house where she thrust them into the wardrobe.

It took three trips to return everything, by which time her anger level had moved up a notch or two.

For a moment she almost decided against dinner, except she was hungry, and, besides, she refused to give in to a fit of the sulks. It wasn't her style.

Steve was tending a barbecue on the terrace when she joined the men. Steaks on the grill smelt delicious, and there were salads to choose from, together with crunchy bread rolls.

Tina took a small steak, added a serve from each salad, and crossed to Nic's side, intent on playing the part of polite wife. 'How was Melbourne?'

'An urgent trip at Paul's request.' A smile curved the edges of his mouth. 'You were asleep when I left.'

'No problems, I hope?' Should she care?

'A few minor hiccups which needed sorting out in private.'

A stand-alone outdoor gas-fired heating unit gave off warmth, tempering the cool evening air, and she watched the light flicker across Nic's strong features, highlighting the angles and planes, the broad cheek-bones.

'As from tomorrow, I want you to use the four-wheel drive.'

'I have a perfectly good car of my own.' One she'd chosen with care, loving the bright yellow paintwork, the sunroof, and the ease of driving, parking.

The very classy, stylish Porsche sitting in the garage wasn't *her*, and she said so.

'Take it,' Nic directed. The vehicle's specs possessed plenty of grunt, lightning acceleration, plus protection and safety. It would also help maintain his peace of mind in caring for her.

'And if I don't?'

Hell, she was a piece of work. 'You want to argue?'

'You want meek compliance?'

He was torn between laughing, or shaking her.

Instead he resorted to drawled cynicism. 'Heaven forbid.'

'Just so we've got that straight.'

Steve busied himself with clearing the barbecue, and when they finished the food Tina gathered up plates, utensils and took them through to the kitchen.

'I'll do that.' Steve had followed her in, and she shook her head.

'You cooked, I get to clean. Go do the man-talk thing with Nic.'

'He's on a call.'

'So take a break. I can rinse and load the dishwasher.'

He lifted both hands in a gesture of mock self-defence and backed off. 'Okay. But when you're done, I get to introduce you to the dog.'

Dog? Impossible it might be a cute, fluffy little house dog she could hug. Visions of a Bichon Frise came to mind, a miniature poodle...

'What breed?' Alsatian, Doberman—

'German Shepherd.'

Tina offered a stunning smile. 'Of course.' Then felt remorse. Steve had done nothing to deserve a facetious response. 'Does it have a name?'

'Czar.'

Another male. She was surrounded by them. 'Give me five minutes.'

He was a beautiful animal, strong, receptive, intelligent. She fell instantly in love, and delighted when the admiration appeared mutual.

'Let's take a walk, shall we?'

Well-trained, Czar obeyed every command, and

gazed at her adoringly when she complimented him and held out her hand…which he immediately licked, then offered a front paw. She laughed, an uninhibited, genuine sound as she fondled his ears. 'You're just gorgeous.'

'And yours.'

Tina sobered and spared Steve a steady look. 'Another protective measure?'

'It bothers you?'

Maybe because until weeks ago her life had revolved around her work, leisure, and sporting pursuits. It had been a good existence, she had been happy, there had been satisfaction in running a successful business that she loved.

Now, by misadventure, she was pregnant with Vasili's child, married to his brother, and under possible threat from her husband's former mistress.

'That's something of an understatement.'

They walked in unison around the perimeter.

'The friendship between you and Nic…'

'Where, when and how?' Steve anticipated.

'Yes.'

'New York, ten years ago, through mutual friends.'

'Succinct.'

'It's my Navy SEAL training.'

She looked at him. 'That clarifies it.'

'Thought it would.'

Together they turned towards the house, where Steve bade her goodnight before retracing his steps.

To his rooms above the garage? A further exercise with Czar?

Tina checked her watch as she ascended the stairs.

A leisurely shower, followed by an early night with a good book seemed a reasonable way to end the day, and with that in mind she entered her suite, crossed into the *en suite*…and stopped.

The toiletries she'd set out on the vanity table were no longer in evidence.

Nic wouldn't have shifted her things *again*, surely?

A quick inspection of the walk-in robe clarified that he had. The chest of drawers had also been emptied.

Damn him!

Anger rose like a tide as she turned and stormed to the master suite and began gathering up her clothes. When she turned, he was standing inside the room.

'Going somewhere?'

She wanted to hit him, and would have if her arms hadn't been filled with clothing. 'Don't you get it? I'm not sleeping in this room with you.'

Nic pushed hands into the front pockets of his jeans and lifted his shoulders in an imperceptible shrug. 'You want to waste time and energy…' He left the words hanging in the air. 'For every time you take those to the guest suite—' he inclined his head towards the clothes she held '—I'll bring them back again.'

She lifted her chin and shot him a dark glare. 'It'll be interesting to see who tires first.'

'Indeed.' He watched with a degree of musing irritation as she walked around him and disappeared through the doorway.

Nic wasn't there when she returned minutes later, and she scooped lingerie out of drawers, balanced toiletries, cosmetics, and managed without anything slipping to the carpeted floor.

Third time round and she was done, and she muttered beneath her breath as she restored everything. Of all the male chauvinistic… Words failed her.

Well, that wasn't strictly true, Tina dismissed as she adjusted the water temperature and stepped into the tiled cubicle. She had a repertoire of unflattering descriptives she'd like to rain on his unsuspecting head.

The warm beat of water began to soothe her temper, and she stayed there, enjoying the feel of water cascading over her body.

It was a while before she turned off the dial and caught up a towel, blotted the moisture from her skin, and tugged a brush through her hair. She reached out a hand for her nightshirt, then cursed beneath her breath when she discovered she hadn't brought it into the *en suite*.

In one swift movement she wrapped the towel, sarong-fashion, around her slim curves and emerged into the bedroom to find her nemesis leaning a hip against the chest of drawers.

'Looking for something?'

If he'd taken her clothes…

She closed her eyes, then slowly opened them again. 'You're enjoying this, aren't you?'

'Not particularly.'

Her eyes flashed green fire. 'I want to *kill* you.'

One eyebrow lifted in silent mocking query. 'You're not exactly dressed for fighting.'

Tina launched herself at him, and cried out as he scooped her into his arms and carried her from the room. She aimed a fist at his shoulder and felt it connect. 'Put me down, you fiend!'

'Soon.'

Tina lifted a fist for a second attack.

'Don't.'

It came as a dangerously silky warning that gave her the sense to pause. Seconds later he released her down onto the carpeted floor in his suite.

She was a tightly coiled feminine ball of fury, with her hair a mass of damp curls, bare shoulders and legs, and a towel that was in danger of slipping low.

'You might want to hitch that towel.'

His musing drawl had her reaching to fasten the edges in double-quick time, and she was helpless against the warmth colouring her cheeks.

It was a long time since he'd seen a woman blush. Most women in his social circle were adept at attracting a man's interest. Subtle flirting was a game they played well, and he recognised all the sophisticated moves.

'I don't want to be here.'

'You can choose,' Nic began with silky indolence, 'between this bed and mine.'

She fought for control, and managed it…barely. 'I hate you.'

'So you've already said.' He raked fingers through his hair and regarded her steadily. 'I have to tend to some paperwork.' He paused for a few seconds. 'Don't plan a repeat trip to the other side of the house. I'll only fetch you back, and then you won't have a choice.'

The thought of spending another night anchored to

his bed was sufficient for her to decide it was infinitely wise to comply.

Tomorrow, however, was another day, offering a further battle.

On the edge of sleep a tiny voice teased...*But who will win the war?*

It was late when Nic re-entered the room. The lights were dimmed low, but not sufficiently low that he couldn't see the small feminine figure curled up in the smaller of the two beds.

She didn't move, except for the steady rise and fall of her breathing, and he let his gaze roam over her delicate features, the cream-textured skin, the slightly parted mouth.

Beautiful, he acknowledged silently. Individual, fiercely independent, with an inner strength that was admirable. Vulnerable, he added, aware of the unusual mix.

He'd consciously chosen to make a life with her. Because of the child she carried. Yet that wasn't strictly true. He'd been intrigued and challenged by her, captivated in a way that surprised him.

There was a part of him that wanted to soothe the pain in her past; to rebuild her trust and have her view him as her friend. Explore what the future might hold.

Something that would take time.

Control...he had it.

And he was a very patient man.

CHAPTER EIGHT

TINA woke to the sound of the shower running. It took a second's orientation to realise where she was. Not her suite. Nic's. Mercifully, not his bed.

The push-pull contretemps of the previous evening came back to haunt her, and she grimaced a little.

What time was it?

Sufficiently early, she determined, not to have to rise for another twenty minutes. However, there was no way she wanted to be *here* when Nic returned from his shower.

She slid to her feet, quickly gathered up fresh underwear, shrugged into a towelling robe, crossed to the empty *en suite* and she didn't emerge until she was showered, partly dressed and her make-up complete, bar lipstick.

Nic was in the process of fixing his tie, and she met and held his steady gaze.

Act, she bade herself silently. You can do it. 'Hi.'

He looked far too *male* for her peace of mind. Dark tailored trousers, the white shirt emphasising his breadth of shoulder, the inherent vitality he managed to exude without any seeming effort.

A power to be reckoned with in the boardroom.

And in the bedroom?

She didn't want to think about it.

A smile teased the edges of his mouth. 'Sleep

well?' He had, knowing she was within reaching distance.

'Yes.' There was surprise, for she couldn't recall waking. With that she disappeared into the walk-in robe, part-closed the door, selected a smart business suit and finished dressing.

Minutes later she caught up her bag, laptop, keys, and made her way down to the kitchen.

'Nic's already left. An early meeting,' Steve explained as she set about organising her own breakfast.

She felt surprisingly well rested. It was Monday, the sun was shining, and the week lay ahead. Another delivery of new stock was due in, and she needed to check out autumn catalogues from several European designers on the net.

There was also a need to check her diary and factor in an appointment with her obstetrician.

Czar lay outside the French doors leading onto the terrace, and she crossed to greet him. His magnificent tail thumped in recognition and he sprang into a sitting position.

'You're to take the four-wheel drive,' Steve reminded her as she made ready to leave, and she gave an expressive eye-roll.

'I'd feel more comfortable if I took it for a test-drive before I face the usual morning rush-hour. Tonight?' she cajoled. 'I promise I'll use it tomorrow.'

'Nic—'

'Pass?' She kept on walking before he had a chance to answer.

Traffic seemed heavier than usual as she traversed

the New South Head Road, and it wasn't until she reached the boutique and began collecting her bag and laptop that she noticed the folded sheet of paper she'd discovered tucked beneath her windscreen the previous evening.

An advertisement for local discounted pizza? Buy-a-coffee-get-one-free offer?

She almost scrunched it into a ball ready to bin it, when something—curiosity, instinct?—made her unfold it.

Instead of the expected bulk printing, the page was blank, except for one word scrawled in bright red lipstick. *Bitch*.

Doing the maths was easy.

Sabine. Had to be.

What got to her was that she'd been watched, followed.

For how long? Since the photograph of her sharing dinner with Nic had appeared in the newspaper? Or had it begun when Nic had re-located from Melbourne to Sydney?

For a moment it gave her a creepy feeling, then common sense offered rational thought.

Sabine was unlikely to try anything in public. All Tina had to do was be extra vigilant whenever she was alone.

As to the note…she'd hand it over to Steve tonight.

The day ran to schedule. Lily bubbled with excitement at having met a new man on a blind date with friends.

'He's nice,' Lily relayed dreamily.

Nice was good. 'I'm happy for you.'

'Thanks. We're taking in a movie tonight.'

Tina was relieved when the day ended and she could close up. A slight edgy feeling had niggled at her composure all day, and she'd found herself checking the entrance each time the electronic door buzzer had sounded, wondering if or when Sabine would show.

She queried the wisdom of asking Lily to stay longer, only to dismiss the request.

For the first time in ages she experienced a feeling of trepidation as she locked up and walked to her car. The area was well lit and there were people around.

Everything went smoothly. No paper tucked beneath the car's windscreen wipers, and no one appeared out of nowhere to surprise her. Although traffic was heavy, no car tailgated her own, nor did anyone follow when she turned into Nic's street.

His Lexus was in the garage when she pulled in, so too was the four-wheel drive.

Paramount was the need to change into something comfortable. Clothing that fitted well was beginning to pull at her waist. And she felt the need for food, a snack, fruit, anything to quell the faint queasiness that seemed to linger.

Nic was in the process of discarding his business suit for jeans when she entered the room, and she quickly averted her attention from the bare muscular chest, powerful thighs, the black hipster briefs...

This room-sharing was going to have to stop. She valued her privacy, and, besides, she'd never survive emotionally if she continued to bump into him at every turn.

'Good day?'

How did she answer that? Go for the kill, or delay a confrontation until after dinner?

'So-so,' Tina managed cautiously as she mentally weighed her options, and she was unprepared when he crossed the room and caught hold of her chin, tilting it so she had no choice but to look at him.

'Explain *so-so*.'

He'd pulled on jeans, which was a relief, although the wide expanse of lightly tanned musculature up close did nothing to prevent the way her pulse jumped to a rapid beat.

'Can we save the report until after dinner? I'd like to change, then eat first.'

Some expression moved across those dark eyes, but she was unable to pin it down. 'Five minutes. The condensed version,' he bade silkily.

'I'm not going to share this suite with you. Someone left a note on my windscreen.'

'Sharing isn't negotiable. Explain the note.'

'In a word—*bitch*.'

He brushed a thumb along her jaw-line, and back again, watching her eyes dilate at his touch. He wanted to pull her in, savour that delicious mouth and ease the fine tension darkening her eyes. Almost did, except she'd react like a spitfire, and any ground he might gain would be lost.

'Tell me you didn't throw the paper away.'

'It's in the car.' She moved back a step, relieved when he let her go. 'And I insist on having my room back.'

His gaze seared hers. 'We've already done this.'

'Your house, your rules?' she flung at him.

'Call it what you will.'

Tina uttered a frustrated oath, one that saw his eyebrow lift as she crossed to the walk-in robe.

When she emerged the room was empty, and in a fit of pique she collected her clothing and transferred them. Just for the hell of it.

Dinner had been prepared in advance by Maria, and afterwards at Steve's bidding she caught up the keys to the four-wheel drive, familiarised herself with it, then she took Czar for a walk around the grounds.

It was after nine when she went upstairs to shower and prepare for bed. Of Nic there was no sign, and she didn't know whether to swear or cry when she discovered her clothing had once more been removed.

Give it up. Except it wasn't about winning or losing. But independence...hers.

Yet persistence, in this case, was proving futile.

Besides, she was tired, she no longer felt inclined to fight him...at least, not tonight, and she'd meet whatever tomorrow would bring.

Wondering when Sabine might show her hand next was a game Tina didn't want to play, and although the woman's appearance was inevitable, waiting for it to happen wasn't doing her nervous system any favours.

An invitation to attend a foreign film première didn't exactly thrill her, for her knowledge of French was limited to a few phrases and words, none of which related to any fluidity with the language.

The evening was, however, a social event, with the

proceeds going to a nominated charity. One the Leandros conglomerate supported.

Dress-up time, Tina accepted as she entered the glittering foyer at Nic's side.

His presence drew immediate attention, and she could understand why. Apart from the fact he was the Leandros heir and numbered among the echelon of wealthy benefactors, he possessed an exigent chemistry, which combined with elemental sexuality succeeded in garnering attention. Especially from women.

Attired in a black evening suit, white linen shirt and black bow-tie, he was something else.

Attractive didn't come close, she admitted as she accepted a flute of orange juice from a passing waiter.

Tina had chosen her outfit with care, electing to wear elegant evening trousers with matching camisole and jacket in deep jade green. Jewellery was confined to a diamond drop pendant and matching earrings.

The *in*-crowd, she perceived, recognising several familiar faces. She observed the air-kiss greetings, admired the women's eveningwear, aware she could put a name to most…and tell the difference between a genuine designer original and a copy.

Mixing and mingling was a refined art form, and there were the society doyennes, some of whom delighted in displaying public affection while in private thought nothing of aiming a figurative dagger.

The games people played, Tina mused, and wondered what they were really like when the social masks were removed.

'Having fun?' Nic's amused drawl brought a sparkling response.

'Of course, darling.'

His eyes gleamed with latent humour as he threaded his fingers through her own. 'You're doing so well.'

'Why, thank you.'

Wit and practised charm. Fire and ice. Vulnerability. It was the latter that curled round his heart and tugged a little. For her determination in becoming a survivor.

'Nicos.'

Tina heard the sultry voice, recognised it on some remote level, and turned to face its owner.

Beauty at its zenith, she accorded, and striking in a way few women ever achieved. The gown was Versace, the make-up perfection, and the hair…a waist-length river of dark silk.

Sabine. In person.

It was a public place with numerous guests. Nic would be forced to play *polite*.

Except he barely inclined his head.

Oh, my.

'Aren't you going to introduce me to your wife?' Sabine purred.

Talk about eating a man alive! The woman was having sex with her eyes…if that were possible.

Tina wanted to turn and walk away. Nic's fingers curled round her own, almost as if he sensed her intention.

'We've already met,' Tina managed calmly, hating being placed in such an invidious position.

Sabine spared her the briefest glance. 'Really?'

Dared she confront? 'You visited my boutique last Friday.' Once begun, why not go for broke? 'Followed me on two occasions, and left an inflammatory note on my windscreen.'

'I don't know what you're talking about.'

Yes, you do, Tina concluded silently. 'It'll be interesting if the police match fingerprints on the note to your own.'

Not so much as an eyelash moved on those exquisite features. 'Jealousy is such an unattractive trait,' Sabine opined with saccharine sweetness.

'Yes, isn't it?' The *touché* was deliberate, and Sabine's eyes narrowed for an instant before she turned her attention to Nic.

'I'm quite disappointed you haven't answered my calls, darling.'

'Why would I do that?'

His voice was as cold as an arctic floe, and Tina suppressed a slight shiver at the thought he might ever use that tone with her. Quiet, deadly, *lethal*.

'We have a history.' Sabine laid a lacquered nail on the sleeve of his jacket, and offered a seductive pout as he removed it.

'You possess a vivid imagination.' His chilling disregard would have cut another woman to shreds. Except Sabine appeared to be immune.

The pout increased. 'Should I go into detail in front of your wife?'

'It would be a wasted effort,' Tina ventured in a deceptively soft voice. 'You see, I don't *care* about Nic's past, or what he did with whom.'

'How remarkably...generous of you.'

'Isn't it?' she parried sweetly, and complied as Nic drew her away.

'I didn't need rescuing.' The protest was genuine, and he lifted their joined hands to his lips.

'It was going nowhere.'

Sensation spiralled from deep within, heating the blood in her veins as it encompassed her body. A sweet, bewitching sorcery that stroked her nerve-ends and brought them to quivering life.

It wasn't fair. She didn't want to feel like this. Couldn't *afford* to, she amended. Needing him would be akin to a living death…a place she refused to visit, even briefly.

At that moment the buzzer sounded as a reminder for guests to take their seats, and Tina looked forward to the cinema's dimly lit auditorium, for then she could relax in the knowledge there was no need to maintain a façade.

Surely Sabine hadn't been able to organise a reserved seat close by. Heaven forbid it might be next to their own.

The seats quickly filled, none of which within immediate proximity appeared to be occupied by Sabine.

Subtitles provided a translation as the film got under way, although the actors' lip synchronicity didn't match, and provided a slight distraction.

Tina became so fascinated by the pathos of unrequited love, the gestures and body language, that it was several minutes before she realised Nic's fingers remained entwined with her own. Something she attempted to rectify, except his hold tightened imperceptibly, making it difficult for her to slip her hand free.

A further attempt was equally unsuccessful, and she pressed her nails against his knuckles in silent warning. To no avail.

So what was the big deal? Maintaining her equilibrium, for one thing.

There was no intermission, and, instead of a happy-ever-after ending, the couple parted and went their separate ways.

'You didn't enjoy it?' They reached the main lobby and began moving towards the main entrance.

'Different to what I expected. Very *noir*.'

'Instead of light and happy with all ends nicely resolved?' Nic teased.

'Of course. However, the cinematography was good.'

There was no sign of Sabine as they made the pavement, nor did she make an appearance as they walked to their car.

Gone, but not forgotten, Tina surmised, and wondered what the woman's next move would be…and when.

'I think you owe me an explanation,' she began as Nic eased the four-wheel drive into the stream of traffic.

He spared her a quick glance. 'Sabine?'

'Who else?'

'We met through mutual friends, shared dinner, met up again at a party. After that she began appearing at whatever social function I happened to attend.' He paused as he negotiated an intersection.

'You shared a relationship with her.'

'For a short time.'

'Which you ended.'

He didn't attempt to disguise the facts. 'It proved difficult.'

Tina could only imagine. She persisted. 'Phone calls, text messages, invitations…all of which you ignored. Then the stalking began,' Tina surmised as she took in the scene beyond the windscreen.

The sky was a dark indigo sprinkled with stars, with the promise of a fine day in sight.

'Did any of that feature in your decision to—?'

'Marry you? No.'

Should she be relieved? The jury was out on that one.

'Sabine wants you.' Is obsessed with you, she added silently.

'I'm taken.'

Now why did that generate a swirl of emotion? It was crazy, *insane* to fall prey to the sensual heat this man managed to project without any effort at all.

All evening he'd been close, too close for comfort. His cologne acted as a sensory aphrodisiac, teasing her senses, creating wanton thoughts that had no place in her life.

She wanted to maintain control…over her emotions, her well-guarded heart. If she lost it, there was no one to catch her when she fell.

'In a marriage that's merely a sham.'

'One which suits both of us.'

Did it? She was no longer so sure.

As Nic drove through the gates the lights came on

in the house, welcoming them home. It was…comforting, Tina admitted as they entered the lobby.

'Go on up,' Nic bade. 'I need to check emails. Time difference,' he added in explanation.

It was an hour before he climbed the stairs and entered their suite. For a moment he wondered if she'd enforced independence and retreated to the other side of the house. Yet the bed next to his own was occupied, her slender frame curled beneath the covers.

She looked defenceless in sleep, her features pale against the rich auburn hair spread over the pillow, and he fought down the urge to slip beneath the covers and gather her in.

Except such an action would bring her sharply awake and heap feminine ire on his head. It would also lose him any ground he'd been able to gain.

CHAPTER NINE

THERE was a sense of relief apparent when the day reached its end without mishap. Business at the boutique had been brisk, the drive home didn't give Tina cause for concern, nor did it faze her to learn Nic was entertaining business associates over dinner in the city.

Home *late* could mean anything. She decided to walk Czar around the garden before fixing a salad and, after eating, taking a shower then sliding into bed with a book. She read for a while, then closed the light and fell into a deep, dreamless sleep from which she didn't wake until morning.

Nic was seated at the breakfast table when she entered the kitchen, and he glanced up and shot her a level look as she moved between refrigerator and counter in easy synchronised movement. Yoghurt, fruit, toast and tea. The latter two first, in case her stomach decided to play revolt.

'Successful night?' Tina posed as she drew out a chair and joined him.

He looked rested, energised, and incredibly male in dark tailored trousers, blue pinstriped shirt and tie. A jacket lay folded over an empty chair.

His smile was vaguely cynical. 'We managed to iron out a few kinks and agree to disagree on a few aspects.'

116

His subtle cologne teased her senses. 'So-so, huh?'

'It could have been better,' he alluded drily.

There was no time like the present. 'Are you free this evening?'

Nic leaned back in his chair and regarded her with a degree of curiosity. 'What do you have in mind?'

The toast was good, so too was the tea. And her stomach appeared to behave. 'Dinner at the Ritz-Carlton,' she elaborated, adding, 'I don't welsh on a bet.'

'Our date.'

Tina silently awarded him high marks for instant recall. 'On condition I get to drive, order, pay, then deliver you home.'

'Role reversal?' She amused him as no other woman did.

'Are you going to object?'

'Not at all.'

Tina checked her watch, gathered up the tub of yoghurt, fruit, then she rose to her feet. 'I'll make a booking. Will seven suit you?'

'Of course.'

She collected her bag, laptop and balanced both as she walked to the door. 'Tonight.'

It would, Nic decided as he shrugged into his jacket and prepared to follow her, prove an interesting evening.

He was waiting for her in the entrance lobby as she descended the stairs shortly after six-thirty, wearing a multi-layered chiffon dress in a subtle floral pattern. Her hair was swept high with a few loose tendrils curling either side of her face, and her only jewellery was a pair of stunning drop earrings.

'I do like punctuality in a man,' Tina managed as she reached him. 'Shall we leave?'

Nic extended an arm. 'After you.'

Choices, she mused as they entered the garage. She'd prefer her Volkswagen, but she doubted it would comfortably accommodate his lengthy frame.

The four-wheel drive won out, and she released the alarm, opened the passenger door and indicated he should get in.

'Isn't this taking role reversal too far?' he drawled as she slid in behind the wheel.

'I promise I won't embarrass your masculinity in public,' she said solemnly, and heard his husky chuckle.

'Thank heaven for small mercies.'

Parking at the Ritz-Carlton wasn't a problem. She simply drove into the entrance and requested valet parking.

The restaurant was well booked, with several guests occupying bar space, and given the choice Tina opted to be taken directly to their reserved table where, once seated, she conferred with the wine steward, requested Nic's preference, and ordered accordingly.

'You've done this before,' Nic said, and watched as she inclined her head.

'Of course.'

'Let me guess,' he ventured lightly. 'Vasili was your partner in crime.'

'True.' She sobered a little, remembering the fun

they'd shared, the laughter in playing the flirting game.

The wine steward delivered the wine and went
through his little spiel, allowing *sir* to sample a taste
when *madam* declined.

When it came to the menu, she dutifully perused it,
suggested a starter, and provided an experienced rundown on the selection of mains.

'May I have some bread?'

She almost laughed at Nic's deferential tone. 'Naturally. Herb, garlic, bruschetta, Turkish?'

'Turkish, I think, with hummus?'

Tina summoned the waiter and placed the order.

'You're getting a kick out of this,' Nic declared,
and met the vaguely impish expression evident in her
eyes.

'And you're not?'

'It provides a refreshing change.'

'I'm glad you're enjoying yourself.'

He wanted to laugh, and settled for a soft chuckle.
'You really intend to see this through?'

Tina inclined her head as bread was brought to the
table.

'Tell me about a day in the life of Nic Leandros.'

'The man, or corporate executive?'

She lifted her glass and took a sip of chilled water.
'The latter.' The *man* was ever-present, invading her
thoughts, her dreams, her life. Too close, too much.

She no longer possessed a safety net, and she'd
never felt so exposed in her life.

'Meetings, in and out of the office. Conference
calls, decisions,' he drawled, watching her expressive

features. 'Dealing with hiccups, delays, the frustrations associated with differing time zones around the world.'

Associates, managers, personal assistants, secretaries...some of whom had to be women. Attractive? Did they have a *thing* for the boss, flirt with him? Aim for something more?

'Yes,' Nic agreed with drawled indolence. 'And no.'

Tina arched a deliberate eyebrow. 'Not for the want of trying, I imagine.' She too could play the mind-reading game.

The waiter delivered their starter, and Tina ate with relish. Lunch had been a snatched bite of a sandwich as and when she could manage it.

'Your turn.'

She dealt with a succulent slice of stuffed mushroom, and followed it with a sip of water. 'A day in the life of Tina—' She almost said 'Matheson'. 'Leandros?' Nearly a *faux pas*.

'Pleasant clients,' she continued. 'Picky customers, delayed deliveries, unavailable stock. The occasional shoplifting attempt,' she added, recalling a few. 'And handling the customer who buys an outfit, wears it that night, then returns it the next day with the excuse it's not suitable and demands a credit.'

'The mantra "the customer is always right" doesn't apply?'

'Not when the customer has been photographed wearing the outfit in public,' she elaborated drily.

The food was divine, and they took their time, en-

joying the ambience, the music filtering softly in the
background.

During the main course Tina brought up the subject
of travel, countries she'd visited, those she'd like to
explore.

'Paris is to die for,' she offered wistfully. 'Austria,
skiing. London. Milan for the fashion shows,' she
added. 'Venice, Rome. New York.' She cast him an
enquiring glance. 'I guess you travel so frequently it's
no longer an adventure. Just long flights, hotel suites,
intense business meetings, with little or no time out
for social activities or pleasure.'

He took a sip of wine, then reached for water. 'That
pretty much covers it.'

'Wheeling and dealing, surviving the vicious cut
and thrust of it all?'

'Yes.'

'You don't take a break…ever?' she queried. 'One
that involves little or no contact with the business
world?'

'Rarely.'

'All work and no play?'

The corners of his mouth twitched with humour.
'You want details of *play*?'

Affairs? There had to be a few. He bore the look
of a man who *knew* women and had bedded many.
The thought disturbed her more than she imagined
possible.

'I doubt you can remember them all,' she managed
sweetly, and heard his quiet laughter.

'You think there have been so many?'

'I'd rather not answer that on the grounds that anything I say…' She let her voice trail deliberately, smiled graciously as the waiter appeared to remove their plates, then she requested the dessert menu and perused it.

'If you have a sweet tooth, the sticky date pudding is to—'

'Die for?'

'Mmm,' Tina agreed with a sunny smile. 'I'm going to settle for the fresh fruit compote.'

They took their time over coffee…tea, in Tina's case, and when the waiter presented the bill she preempted him by indicating it should be given to her.

'If you insist.' Nic's voice held mild amusement, and she spared him a severe glance as she tendered her credit card.

Minutes later she signalled the concierge to collect the four-wheel drive.

'Thank you for a pleasant evening,' Nic said with unruffled ease as she drew the vehicle to a halt in the garage.

'You're welcome.'

They entered the house together, and she made for the stairs.

'You forgot something.'

She turned, faint surprise etching her features as he moved towards her.

'Isn't this where you get to kiss me goodnight?'

He was kidding…wasn't he?

Tina hesitated, then reached up and pressed her lips to his cheek. At least that was her intention. Except he moved and her mouth connected with his own.

He didn't allow her the opportunity to pull back.

Instead he captured her head between both hands and took her fleeting touch and turned it into something more.

Much more. A slow, exploratory dance, wholly sensual...dazzling in its intensity. A taste of passion, electrifying and as intoxicating as fine vintage champagne.

Dear heaven, she registered on some deep level. If this was how he kissed, what would it be like if he made love?

Don't go there.

She had no idea how long it lasted. Thirty seconds, a hundred...more.

When he released her she could only stand there looking at him in stunned silence.

He trailed gentle fingers down her cheek and let them rest fleetingly on her mouth. 'Sleep well.'

She remained standing there as he turned towards the study, and it was only when she heard the imperceptible click of the door closing that she made her way to their suite.

Sleep was never more distant. Her lips, her mouth...dammit, her entire body was incandescent with sensual heat.

It wasn't fair.

Work provided a necessary distraction, and with each passing day Tina became a little more at ease in sharing the large master suite.

It helped that there were two *en suites*, two spacious walk-in robes. Individual privacy could be maintained...and was, she reflected with relief.

Although living in such close proximity meant she

was constantly aware of his presence. The thrown-back covers on his large bed, the clothes he'd worn during the day draped over a valet frame. The faint lingering scent of his cologne. The fresh smell of soap drifting from his *en suite* after each shower.

The occasional glimpse of him in a state of semi-undress was enough to send her pulse racing to a rapid beat.

Tonight wasn't any different as she put the finishing touches to her make-up, then crossed into her walk-in robe to dress.

Nic stood, naked from the waist up as he pulled on trousers. One glance was all it took for her nerve-ends to go completely haywire. Gleaming tanned skin stretched over strong muscles that flexed with every move he made.

At that moment he lifted his head and their eyes locked, fused for a few infinitesimal seconds. Then he smiled, and every bone in her body went into serious meltdown.

No one man deserved to look so ruggedly attractive, or effortlessly project more than his fair share of sexual chemistry. Primitive, intensely sensual. Lethal.

Tina forced herself to utter a casual, 'Won't be long,' before disappearing into the walk-in robe.

The gown she'd chosen to wear was a dream in deep blue chiffon silk, with a beaded fitted bodice, spaghetti straps, and a layered skirt. There was a matching beaded jacket to complete the outfit, and she slid her feet into hand-crafted stilettos, then added the finishing touch of delicate diamond drop earrings.

With a few dextrous strokes she fixed a few stray

tendrils of hair, then she crossed into the bedroom to discover Nic standing indolently at ease, looking, she determined, far too compelling for any woman's peace of mind.

Especially hers.

'Ready to go?'

Tina caught up her evening purse and offered him a stunning smile. 'Showtime.'

'There's just one thing.'

He crossed to her side and she resorted to humour as a defence mechanism. 'Lipstick on my teeth? Smudged mascara?'

'You look beautiful.' A beauty that came from within, he added silently.

Oh, my. Did he have any idea how he affected her?

'Thank you.' She let her eyes skim his impeccably suited frame. 'Believe you'll have the women vying for your attention in droves.'

'You're verging on overkill.'

She shot him a witching smile as they descended the stairs. 'Really?'

Traffic was heavy as they made their way into the inner city and joined a queue of cars lining up for valet parking at the prestigious hotel.

The Royal Children's Hospital benefit was a glittering annual event, patronised by many and attended to capacity, Tina mused as she stood beside Nic in the foyer of the hotel's grand ballroom.

Anyone who was *someone* was there, and she recognised a few society doyennes, the titled few, and some of her clientele.

The women wore designer gowns, a ransom in jewellery, while the men looked resplendent in black suit and bow-tie.

Waitresses plied guests with champagne and orange juice, and the muted music was almost eclipsed by the buzz of conversation as guests mixed and mingled.

Premonition or a finely tuned instinct? Tina wondered silently as her gaze idly skimmed the room.

Would Sabine make a last-minute appearance?

The charity had been booked out for weeks, and the only way Sabine could gain entrance was an ability to persuade an existing ticket holder to part with their own.

At that moment doors to the huge ballroom were thrown open, guests were invited to take their seats, and Tina allowed herself an inward sigh of relief as they reached their reserved table.

Ill-timed, given Sabine's appearance scant minutes before the Master of Ceremonies took the podium.

The woman's magnificent hair stood her apart from every other woman in attendance. If that wasn't sufficient to garner notice, Sabine had chosen to wear black…a strapless backless creation that moulded her perfect curves. The effect was so exceptionally stunning it doubtlessly quickened every man's pulse…as well as another part of their male anatomy.

Scarlet lipstick and gloss, matching lacquered nails, Sabine epitomised the ultimate sexy seductress.

Her male handbag for the evening was a polished escort whose model looks and body probably came at a high price.

There were two vacant chairs at an adjacent table,

and Tina watched with idle fascination as Sabine slowly threaded her way towards them.

Amazingly, the Master of Ceremonies delayed beginning his speech until Sabine and her companion were seated.

There was no one word in any dictionary to do Sabine justice.

Worse, Sabine sat directly in Tina's line of vision. A line of vision Nic also shared.

It was, Tina concluded, going to be one hell of an evening.

An understatement, for Sabine played every trick in the book...and then some. Without doubt solely for Nic's benefit.

A reminder of what he'd shared...and still could?

Tina told herself she didn't care.

Instead, she sipped chilled water, forked small morsels of food into her mouth with no recollection of their taste or texture.

She also conversed with fellow guests sharing their table. Although afterwards she could remember neither the topic nor her contribution.

The faint niggling back pain that had persisted on and off through the day suddenly intensified into a deep spreading ache, and she subtly shifted a little in the hope of easing it.

Had she slept awkwardly? Inadvertently stretched a muscle? It couldn't be something she'd eaten, surely?

Perhaps it would help if she stood up and moved a little. A visit to the powder-room?

It took a while, as several other women guests decided to take advantage of a lull in the evening's proceedings.

Coffee had already been served when she finally re-entered the ballroom, and various guests were exchanging seats at different tables while others made slow progress towards the main doors.

Tina bore Nic's swift appraisal as she slid into her seat. 'Time to leave?'

'Please.'

His gaze sharpened as he took in her pale features, the darkness lurking in those beautiful green eyes. 'What is it?'

If only it were something as simple as a headache, but she was afraid it was more than that. 'I'm not sure.'

Nic didn't hesitate as he made a swift call to the concierge, then he led her out to the lobby where their car was already waiting for them.

'I'd rather go home first,' Tina protested as Nic headed for the nearest private hospital. The next instant a spasm of pain temporarily suspended her breathing, and any doubt she might have had gave way to sickening certainty.

Everything after that became a blur as she was wheeled into the emergency ward, admitted, questioned, put on an intravenous drip, then examined.

Miscarriage, or spontaneous abortion as it was termed. Quite common. They'd run some tests, do a scan, give her pain relief, and check her throughout the night. All being well, she'd be released late tomorrow.

'Go home,' Tina directed when Nic remained after the medics were done.

His expression was bleak, his eyes dark and unfathomable as he pulled a chair close to the bed. 'I'm staying.'

'You can't.'

'Watch me.'

She felt too drained to argue with him, and she simply closed her eyes, unwilling to think. Not *wanting* to think as she began to drift. Had they given her something to make her sleep? What *time* was it?

Dammit…what did it matter? *Nothing* mattered any more.

Uninterrupted sleep was an impossibility as nursing staff seemed to appear at frequent intervals through what remained of the night. Once, when she turned her head to check, Nic was still there.

The hospital's quietness was broken with the early morning nursing shift change, the appearance of the tea lady, and general fussing in preparation for the various doctors' rounds.

Of Nic there was no sign, and when she queried she was told he'd gone home to change.

Tina showered and put on a fresh hospital gown, then, at the nurse's urging, slid back into bed.

'Are you comfortable, dear? Breakfast will be served soon.'

There was a remote unit to activate the television set mounted high on the wall. Magazines to choose from. She wasn't interested in either, but anything was better than reflecting on the miscarriage.

It was as if she was locked into a state of ambivalence, where few or no emotions existed.

Another nurse breezed in, took her temperature, checked her blood pressure, the intravenous drip, then asked how she felt.

'Fine.' The blank answer was automatic. The truth was she didn't know how she felt.

Her mind was whirling with thoughts. There was vague guilt that the pregnancy had been a mistake; not a planned event conceived out of mutual consent and longing for a child. She recalled her initial shock, decisions, Vasili's accidental death. Tina's head spun with it all, her thoughts intensifying as she remembered Nic's insistence that they share a marriage of convenience for the sake of the Leandros heir.

Except now there was no child.

So where did that leave her?

Breakfast arrived, and she picked at it, choosing fruit and cereal, toast, then drank the tea.

Tina glanced up and saw Nic framed in the door for an instant, then he crossed to the bed and leaned down to brush his lips to her forehead.

'How are you?'

He'd changed into tailored trousers, open-necked shirt and jacket. He indicated the holdall in one hand. 'I've brought you some clothes. Things I thought you might need.' He had flowers, an enormous sheaf of them. 'The nurse said she'd find a vase.'

'Thanks.'

She looked…fragile. And her eyes held shadows he could only begin to guess at. 'I checked at the nurses' station. The obstetrician will be here soon.'

'So they said.'

He beat the urge to collect her from the bed, settle with her in the chair and hold her close. Except she'd probably resist the move. His eyes locked with hers, but she was the first to look away.

Hell. Did she know how helpless he felt? How words…any words…seemed inadequate?

The obstetrician came and went, organised a follow-up consultation, and sanctioned her discharge later in the day.

She could go home.

A good suggestion…except, where was home *now*?

No pregnancy meant there was no need for the marriage to continue. When could she expect Nic to file for divorce? For divorce was inevitable…wasn't it?

'I've made a few necessary calls,' Nic relayed quietly. 'Lily will take charge of the boutique, and Claire will be here around midday. I've invited her to stay for a few days. Stacey will call you tonight.'

Claire? There had never been a time when she'd needed her mother more.

Nic remained until it was time to go and collect Claire from the airport and he brought her directly to the hospital.

Tina held out her arms and enfolded her mother close. 'It's so good to see you.' She patted the bed. 'Sit.'

Nic smiled at the sight of them, two women who looked more like sisters than mother and daughter.

'I'll go leave you to it.' He leaned in and brushed his lips to Tina's cheek. 'Be back at four.'

'Thanks,' she said quietly.

It was wonderful to catch up with her mother, and they talked up a storm…about everyone and everything, except the most pressing aspect of all. How the miscarriage would affect her relationship with Nic.

Tina found it impossible to put her fears into words, and Claire, with a mother's intuition, left the subject well alone.

'How long are you staying?'

'Until Tuesday. I'll get the late flight back, stay in Brisbane overnight, and leave for Noosa at dawn.'

Two days. It wasn't long enough, and she said so.

Dinner that evening was a convivial meal. Steve had outdone himself with a superb roast chicken and various salads, and he produced a delicious cheesecake, which he admitted he'd collected from a local bakery.

There was coffee, and Tina savoured it with the appreciation of one denied the pleasure for several weeks. A tiny bonus, but one nonetheless. And right now, she'd take any bonus she could get.

Stacey's call, when it came, proved difficult for them both. There were no *right* words, nothing to ease Stacey's pain of a double loss within a matter of weeks. It served to intensify Tina's guilt…unfounded, she knew, but there nonetheless. Not only for the loss of the child, but the fear of losing Nic.

'Darling, why don't you go up to bed?' Claire suggested gently around nine. 'I can't imagine you had much sleep last night.'

'You just want to get rid of me, so you can charm these two men,' she teased, and heard her mother's light laugh.

'How did you guess?'

Nic rose to his feet in one easy movement and accompanied her into the foyer.

'You don't need to come with me,' she said quietly. 'I'm not going to fall in a heap between here and the bedroom.'

Inner strength and fragility. It was her fragility that threw him, for he could see her closing up, distancing herself, and he felt powerless to prevent it.

'No,' he agreed with studied ease as he began ascending the stairs at her side.

They reached the upper floor and traversed the hallway to the master suite.

Inside Tina turned to face him. 'So why are you here?'

'Ensuring you take prescribed medication.' He crossed into the *en suite*, filled a glass with water and returned to hand her the pills.

'I don't need a nurse.'

'I wasn't aware I suggested you did.' Tina swallowed them down, then watched as he walked to the door.

'I'll be up later.'

Then he was gone.

She was fine, she told herself as she undressed and slid into bed. What was more, she'd read for a while…

When Nic re-entered the room she was asleep, and the book lay on the carpeted floor.

He scooped it up and placed it on the bedside table, then he stood looking down at her for a few minutes as she slept.

The temptation to slide in beside her and gather her close was almost irresistible.

Instead he crossed the room, shed his clothes and slid into his own bed to lay staring at the darkened ceiling as he became locked into contemplative thought.

CHAPTER TEN

'WHAT do you feel like doing today?'

It was after nine, the morning was clear with a hint of spring warmth in the air, and there was a sense of relaxed pleasure in having shared breakfast with Claire and taking the opportunity to enjoy a second cup of coffee without needing to hurry.

'Spending time with you, darling.'

'Why don't we go check out the boutique?' Tina suggested. 'Take in lunch and do a little retail therapy?'

'Cabin fever, so soon?' her mother teased.

'Got it in one.' How could she explain that she had a burning need to get out of this house? A house she might very soon be asked to leave?

'You don't think you should rest?'

Tina shook her head. 'I did that yesterday, remember? At your and Nic's insistence.' With Steve as back-up guard, she hadn't stood a chance. But to-day…well, today was a different matter.

'The obstetrician—'

'Assured me I'm fine to ease back into a normal routine.'

Claire's eyes twinkled a little. 'I'm all too familiar with that determined streak of yours. Four hours, tops,' she cautioned. 'Less, if I think you're beginning to fade.'

They left at eleven, despite Steve's voiced reluctance, with Claire at the wheel and Double Bay as their destination.

The boutique was Tina's first priority, and Lily's delighted greeting and warm hug made her day.

'It's great to see you,' Lily enthused. 'But should you be here?'

'That's what I told her.'

Lily offered Claire a mischievous smile. 'Didn't listen, did she?'

'I have her on a leash.'

'Ready to rein her in?'

'If you don't desist in talking about me as if I'm not here…' Tina protested in a light voice. 'Any problems?'

'None I can't handle,' Lily assured, and reeled off stock deliveries, sales, orders.

'Want to take a break while Claire and I mind shop?'

Claire stepped forward. 'I mind, you sit,' she directed briskly. 'Lily, go take half an hour.'

It was good to be back, Tina mused. Anyone would think she'd been gone weeks instead of a day. Tomorrow she'd come in for several hours, maybe ten-thirty until three-thirty or four. If the going got tough, she could always leave.

'I like what you're doing here,' Claire complimented as she riffled through stock. 'It's well organised and beautifully displayed.'

'Thanks.'

It was pleasant to see her mother work the clients who intended to browse, and bought due to Claire's superb salesmanship. Definitely an art, Tina acknowl-edged, and one her mother possessed in spades.

'I learnt from the best,' she applauded when the boutique emptied, and caught Claire's smile.

'The item looked good, complimented her figure and colouring…it sold itself.'

'Sure.'

They were both smiling when Lily returned, and she offered with a quizzical lift of one eyebrow, 'Are you going to share, or do I have to guess?'

'Claire just sold the Saab ensemble.'

Lily's expression was comical. 'That only went out into stock this morning. Maybe you should stay awhile.'

Claire collected her bag. 'I'm taking my daughter to lunch.'

'Hey,' Tina protested. 'My invitation, my treat.'

'You don't stand a chance, darling. The only de-cision you get to make is the choice of venue.'

Tina glanced from her mother to Lily. 'I'll be in tomorrow.'

'Better check with Nic first,' Lily warned, and ig-nored Tina's expressive eye-roll.

It was early, most of the lunching crowd didn't con-gregate till late in the day, and although reservations were heavy, Tina managed to secure a table at an elegant restaurant well known for its fine cuisine.

They settled on a light main, declined wine, and opted for mineral water.

'Lily seems to be managing very well.' Claire took a sip of water and leant back a little in her chair. 'You could easily take a break away.'

'Maybe.'

'Think about it,' her mother encouraged, and Tina inclined her head, only to dip it quickly on recognition of *whom* the *maître d'* was bent on ushering towards a vacant table.

Sabine.

'Something wrong, darling?'

An understatement, if ever there was one.

'Why, *Tina*.' The soft, purring voice was definitely feline. 'I didn't expect to see you here.'

Believe me, neither did I. 'No,' she managed in a noncommittal tone.

Sabine turned towards Claire. 'I don't think we've met. Sabine Lafarge. An—' she deliberately effected a telling pause '—old friend from Nic's past.'

Not so *old*, and determined to intrude on the present.

'Perhaps I could join you?'

Pushy, definitely pushy, Tina determined and was about to refuse when her mother beat her to it.

'No.'

Ah, Claire hadn't lost her touch for summing up a person in seconds flat.

'The restaurant has no spare tables.'

Tina waited expectantly, and wasn't disappointed with her mother's firm response. 'We're having a private conversation.' Lifting a hand, she summoned the *maître d'*, explained they were not inclined to share and heard his voluble apology.

'But madam insisted she is a friend.'

Claire's smile was pure honey. 'Madam is wrong.'

Sabine's killing gaze held a laser quality as she turned and walked from the restaurant.

'You owe me an explanation,' Claire began evenly.

Tina offered the condensed version, only to see her mother's eyes narrow.

'That's one dangerous female. Watch your back, darling.'

'Watching,' she said obediently. 'More coffee?' Having been denied coffee for several weeks, she seemed bent on making up for lost time.

'Nic's reaction to this is…?' Claire pursued and Tina stifled an inward groan. When Claire took the bit between her teeth, there was no stopping her.

'Tightened security,' she enlightened quietly. 'Steve doubles as a bodyguard. I carry a tracking device. My Volkswagen stays in the garage and I get to drive the fastest, most sophisticated grunt machine on four wheels. There's also a guard dog.' She took a deep breath and expelled it slowly. 'Enough, already?'

'I'm impressed.'

'One can only wonder how long it'll last.'

Claire offered a thoughtful look. 'Because?'

'There's no longer a Leandros heir.'

Her mother appeared to take a moment. Concentrating on a careful assemblage of words, perhaps?

'Is it not feasible at some stage in the future you and Nic might consider having a child together?'

Tina was temporarily lost for words. 'You know—'

'Yes, I do,' Claire said quickly. 'Only too well. I was there, remember?'

'Then why would you—?'

'Suggest it?' Claire posed. 'Isn't there a part of you that wants to love and be loved? To feel secure in a relationship? To grow old with a man who is not only your lover, but your best friend?'

'And as a marriage to Nic already exists, why not kill two birds with one stone?' She couldn't begin to describe how the thought affected her. 'Haven't you forgotten one small detail?' She aimed for calm, and almost didn't make it. 'Maybe that's not what either of us might want?'

Claire looked thoughtful. 'Don't *you*?'

'I don't need the complication.'

That hardly answered the question, but at this point it boded well not to comment, Claire decided, and signalled for the bill. 'Retail therapy?' she suggested with a smile.

They arrived home two hours later with several brightly emblazoned carry-bags, which they had fun separating and re-examining.

Maria had prepared minestrone soup and a delicious lamb roast for dinner, and Tina insisted on preparing the table while Claire retreated upstairs to pack.

Nic entered the dining-room as she placed the last glass, and she stilled the faint fluttering sensation in her stomach as he came close.

'Good day?'

She stood back a pace and offered a slight smile. 'Claire and I checked the boutique, did lunch and engaged in some retail therapy.'

He caught hold of her chin, lifted it, and examined her features. 'You were supposed to rest.'

'I've already done this with Claire.'

Nic decided not to pursue it. 'Any problems?'

He'd hear about it anyway, so she might as well spill it out. 'Sabine entered the same restaurant and did her best to join us.'

His eyes sharpened. 'I gather she was unsuccessful?'

Tina attempted to move free from him, and failed miserably as he cupped her face between both hands.

She didn't want to be this close to him, for all it took was a look at that sensually curved mouth to remember just how it felt on her own. 'Please, I need to go freshen up before dinner.'

He lowered his head and kissed her…a slow, gentle sweep of his tongue over hers, then he let her go.

It was enough he'd felt the quickened pulse-beat, sensed her quick intake of breath an instant before his mouth had settled on her own.

Nic watched her leave the room, then he crossed into the kitchen and conferred with Steve. Today's rebuttal would have increased Sabine's need to strike back. The difficult part was predicting how, when and where.

Steve joined them for dinner, and conversation was kept light as anecdotes were exchanged and commented upon.

Normal, Tina judged as they drove Claire out to the airport.

It was hard to say 'goodbye' when it came time for her mother to pass through to the departure lounge, and Tina fought against a sudden bereft feeling as Claire disappeared from sight.

Tiredness descended like a shroud as Nic drove home, and she simply leaned her head back against the cushioned rest and closed her eyes.

She felt all talked out and incredibly weary.

Did she actually fall asleep? She couldn't be sure.

When Nic brought the car to a halt in the garage she undid her seat belt and preceded him into the house. Bed, she decided. But first a shower.

A muscle bunched at the edge of his jaw as he ascended the stairs at her side, and she uttered a faint protest when he swept an arm beneath her knees.

'I can walk.'

'Indulge me.'

She really didn't want to, but struggling for independence would gain nothing.

'I'm fine,' she assured him as they reached the bedroom.

'Sure you are.' He let her slide down to stand on her feet, and he reached for the buttons on her shirt.

'What do you think you're doing?'

'Undressing you.'

He sounded almost...caring. And despite her tiredness, it put a whole different context on his ministrations. One that caused faint alarm bells as his fingers skimmed her skin.

She didn't want to feel like this. Dammit, to stand here quiescent was a madness she couldn't afford.

'Don't.' Was that her voice? Pleading, almost begging him to desist.

He took little notice and continued with the task until she stood in bra and briefs. 'Go.'

Tina escaped into the *en suite*, and returned a while

later to find the lights dimmed low, her bed turned down, and a glass of water together with two pills on her nightstand, which she ignored. She wasn't in any pain and she didn't need anything to help her sleep.

She'd always thought it a fallacy that anyone could fall asleep the instant their head hit the pillow. Yet all she remembered was closing her eyes.

Later she had no idea of the time or how long she'd been asleep. All she knew was that it was dark, and she was locked into a familiar nightmare…where she was in bed in her apartment, the faint sound, the muffled movement, then the hand clamped over her mouth.

She couldn't breathe, couldn't see, and she began to struggle, fighting against a strength much stronger than her own…

'Tina.'

Strong hands held her flailing arms as a male voice penetrated her subconscious. Yet still she fought him, kicking out in an effort to find any slight advantage in her quest to best him.

Her name sounded clear, close…and the nightmare faded as she returned to the present.

She took in the large room, and experienced a mixture of consternation and relief with the recognition of where she was and with whom.

She had a haunted look, her eyes, wide dark pools, mirrored unspoken terror…and Nic transferred her from her bed into his, in spite of her protest.

'Shut up,' he chastised quietly as he anchored her close. 'Just…shut up.'

She shouldn't be here, shouldn't stay. Except it felt

so *good*. His body was warm, his arms strong, she felt safe. Secure, she amended silently as she gave in and let herself drift.

Tina stirred into wakefulness through the night, moved slightly and became aware she lay curved against a warm, muscular chest. What was more, she was held in position by a strong male arm.

Then she remembered…and felt her senses quicken.

It would be so easy to stay. To snuggle in against him and enjoy the closeness, breathe in his warm male scent, and feel the slide of his hand…

What was she thinking?

She couldn't go where he might lead. Told herself she didn't want to. And knew she lied.

In the night's darkness it was possible to indulge the mind, to allow herself to believe anything was achievable. Even love.

Claire's words whispered through her brain, adding to the fantasy of what her life might be like with Nic, children…a future.

Except it wasn't going to happen.

What was more, to remain in the same bed with him was *impossible*.

She'd die if he stirred in his sleep and mistakenly thought she was someone else, and began making a move on her.

Out, a silent voice urged. *Now.*

The thing, she determined several minutes later, was achieving her escape. Not easy when every inch she gained was lost as the arm draped over her waist tightened.

An involuntary action, or deliberate?

Involuntary, she decided. Had to be.

What next? The bold approach? That might work.

It did, and she slid into her own bed with a sense of relief.

There was no sign of Nic when Tina woke, and she went down to breakfast prepared to do battle regarding her decision to return to work. Only to have Steve relay Nic had already eaten, and was on his way into the city.

'Do you think you should?' Steve queried when she voiced her intention.

Assertiveness was the key. 'Yes.'

'Be alert,' he warned. 'Sabine—'

'May increase the nuisance factor,' she finished for him, and received his succinct confirmation.

'Got it,' Tina assured him as she collected her keys.

The morning proved busy, and there was a sense of normality in slipping back into a familiar routine. The stock looked great; Lily had shown herself to be more than capable in the few days Tina had been absent. Sales receipts were good, there had been one or two minor hiccups…but nothing Lily wasn't able to handle.

Around eleven Lily answered the phone, spoke quietly, then handed Tina the receiver. 'Your gorgeous husband.'

'What do you think you're doing?' His voice was pure silk.

'Working.'

'Ensure it's not for the entire day.'

She wasn't in the mood for over-protectiveness. 'We're busy,' she managed quietly. 'I have to go.'

She cut the connection, cast the salon a quick glance…and realised the day had just taken a turn for the worse.

Sabine. On a mission. With no doubt as to who was her target.

'We need to talk,' the woman began without preamble as she reached the counter.

'There's nothing to discuss,' Tina responded evenly.

Sabine offered a searing look meant to turn her victim to ash. 'Get out of Nicos' life. Or I'll take you out.'

Tina could see Lily surreptitiously keying digits into her cellphone in the background.

'I'd like you to leave,' Tina voiced with deceptive calm, doubtful *polite* would work.

'When I'm done.'

Don't take your eyes from hers. An essential caution.

Yet the attack came out of nowhere, lightning quick and deliberately vicious as Sabine's hand connected with Tina's cheekbone.

'Nic is *mine*,' Sabine hissed as Tina steadied herself.

Without a further word the woman turned and strode to the door…which didn't budge. Whereupon Sabine yelled in fury, 'Open the door.'

'It'll stay closed until the police arrive.'

Sabine turned on Lily. 'Open it!'

The scene could go any which way, but two against one had to provide some advantage.

Sabine's howl of outrage was almost animalistic in tone when Lily didn't move, and in a fit of rage the woman began to run amok through the salon, pushing over an antique cheval-mirror, then she snatched up a bag from display and hurled it at Tina...who ducked, then successfully tackled Sabine to the carpeted floor.

It wasn't the smoothest move. But then the salon wasn't a *dojo* where carefully orchestrated manoeuvres were made with skill and expertise.

Down and dirty was never pretty!

Steve arrived minutes ahead of the police, and everything after that took on an unreal quality.

Tina endured Steve's scrutiny and waved aside his insistence the cut on her cheekbone needed an ice-pack.

She also attempted to avoid being photographed, and was in the midst of voluble protest when Nic entered the salon.

His presence resulted in an outraged plea from Sabine, which he ignored, nor did he offer the woman so much as a glance.

Instead he crossed directly to where Tina stood and subjected her dishevelled form to a sweeping appraisal.

'It's not as bad as it looks,' she managed, aware her hair had escaped from its smooth pleat and was all over the place. Her skirt didn't exactly sit right, her shirt was out and, when she checked, a few buttons were missing.

He took in the cut and swelling on her cheek, the

gouges on her hands from Sabine's lacquered nails, and turned towards the attending officer, offered a few succinct words and added, 'Throw the book at her.'

A bright flash, and Steve had his photograph. It coincided with one the police photographer took of Tina, the fallen cheval-mirror.

'I should go tidy up,' Tina inclined, and it was only when she checked her mirrored image that she realised just what a sight she presented.

Nic's image appeared behind her own, and she offered a token resistance as he turned her to face him.

He lifted a hand and touched her cheek with gentle fingers, saw her wince, and let them trail down to rest at the edge of her mouth.

His eyes were dark, his expression unfathomable, almost as if he didn't trust himself to speak.

She had to say something…anything was better than the silence that stretched between them.

'Sabine finally made a physical move,' Tina offered, and glimpsed a muscle bunch at the edge of his jaw.

'At considerable cost to you.'

'It could have been worse.'

'I'm taking you to get this—' he indicated her swollen cheek '—checked out. Then we're going home.'

She rotated her jaw. 'You want to play nurse…fine. But I'm staying here.' She needed to keep occupied, not spend time on reflection.

'On one condition. Steve stays with you.'

'Isn't that going just a tad overboard?'

'No.'

Tina filched a brush from her bag and tidied her hair, fixed her clothes, retouched her lipstick and returned to the salon in time to see Sabine escorted into a police car.

The salon presented its usual tidy appearance, doubtless due to Lily's efforts, and an officer was busy recording Lily's version of events.

'This is so unnecessary,' Tina voiced as a medic probed her cheek and swabbed the cut.

'You're going to have a beautiful bruise,' came the breezy response.

'I'll put ice on it,' she promised.

'That'll help.'

Then they were out of there, and she turned towards Nic as they reached the boutique. 'Satisfied?'

'No, but it'll keep.'

A police officer had remained to record Tina's account, and he expressed a need to access the boutique's security cameras, explained both Tina and Lily's statements would be ready to sign late that afternoon, then he left.

Nic followed after exchanging a few words with Steve, who in turn indicated he'd remain out back.

'Don't want to frighten the women away.'

Lily put her head to one side and cast him a wicked smile. 'Oh, I don't know. We could camp you up a bit, add some unisex shades, and there you go…we've gained a new assistant.'

'I don't think so.'

'Pity,' Lily teased.

It was fortunate the incident had occurred close to midday when most of their clientele lunched, and Tina downplayed it for those few who expressed curiosity at witnessing police moving in and out of the boutique.

They sent out for lunch and ate during alternate short breaks. Together, they contrived to keep busy, and bade each other an affectionate 'goodnight' at day's end.

Tina drove towards Rose Bay with Steve following close behind. Nic's Lexus was parked inside the garage, and there was nothing she could do about the sensation curling inside her stomach as she ascended the stairs.

It was crazy to feel like this, to be so aware of a man who had taken control of her life, turned it upside down…and was doubtlessly going to pitch her out of *his* life very soon.

The question was when, not if. And waiting for the figurative axe to fall was akin to walking a tightrope with no safety net.

Sabine Lafarge would be dealt with…but how long before a team of lawyers filed for her release on bail? What then?

Tina entered the master suite and came to an abrupt halt at the sight of Nic emerging into the bedroom with a towel hitched at his waist.

His dark hair was damp from his recent shower, and there was too much muscular flesh exposed for her peace of mind.

All it took was a glance for her to vividly recall what it felt like to be held close against him for several hours through the night.

Worse, how much *more* she wanted from him.

To know she could walk up to him and pull his head down to hers, to savour his kiss, initiate intimacy and luxuriate in his response.

The mere thought of him as a lover sent the blood racing through her veins. He had the look, the touch that could drive a woman wild. It was there in his eyes, his stance...a magnetic quality that exuded sensuality at its zenith.

'Hi.' As a greeting it was incredibly inane.

He crossed the room and stood close. Much too close, for she could inhale the clean smell of the soap emanating from his skin.

'Hi, yourself.'

His voice held a teasing quality as he brushed gentle fingers along the edge of her jaw. 'How's the pain threshold?'

'Bearable.' In truth the left side of her face ached.

'In other words, it hurts like hell.' He traced the slope of her nose. 'Take something for it.'

Tina inclined her head and made for the shower, emerging a while later to don tailored trousers and a knit top. She left her hair loose, added moisturiser and pink gloss, then she ran lightly downstairs.

Food...whatever it was smelt good. What was more she was hungry. Which had to be a first for more than a week nursing a lacklustre appetite.

Maria had prepared lasagne, a crisp salad, and there were crunchy bread rolls. Ambrosia, Tina admitted silently as she tucked into her portion.

'Any update on Sabine?'

'Out on bail,' Steve informed. 'Nic has filed

charges, and taken out a Restraining Order on your behalf. You need to confirm and sign your statement.'

'I'll do it on the way to work in the morning.'

'Early,' Nic informed. 'On our way to the airport.'

She was in the process of forking a morsel of lasagne and her action stilled as she cast him a puzzled look. 'Would you care to run that by me again?'

'We're spending a few days on Hayman Island in the Whitsundays.'

Tropical north Queensland. Sunshine, warm temperatures, sandy beaches, clear waters.

'You made this decision…*when*?'

'This afternoon.'

'Had your PA clear your schedule and make bookings?'

'Yes.'

'There's just one thing,' Tina offered solemnly. 'You forgot to ask if *I* could factor in a few days away.'

Nic tore a piece of bread from his roll and ate it. 'It's a done deal,' he relayed with deceptive quietness. 'Lily will take care of the boutique with a little help from her cousin Annie…whom Lily assures me you like and trust.'

She replaced her cutlery with care. 'You achieved this in—' she lifted a hand and clicked thumb and finger together '—a matter of minutes. A few phone calls, an offered bonus…phfft, and it's done.'

He looked vaguely amused. 'Something like that.'

'And if I refuse?'

His gaze hardened. 'I'm not giving you that option.'

'Short of manhandling me onto the flight, how do you expect to get me there?'

One eyebrow rose. 'Opposing me just for the sheer hell of it?'

She sounded ungracious. And heaven knew, she didn't mean to be. It was just…everything. The worst was not knowing what the next step would be.

'No. Unsure whether the two of us together twenty-four hours a day is a good thing.'

'Oh, I don't know,' Nic drawled. 'You might be pleasantly surprised.'

CHAPTER ELEVEN

THERE could be no doubt that in terms of *wanting to get away from it all*, a magnificent private island was the place to be.

The sunshine, clear blue skies and sparkling ocean waters provided a tranquil air.

One Tina coveted as she familiarised herself with the luxury suite they'd been assigned. Splendid views greeted her from wall-to-wall glass doors, shaded in part by bi-fold wooden shutters.

'Thank you.' She turned towards Nic.

'For what, specifically?'

'Bringing me here,' she said quietly. Putting a distance between what the past several weeks represented. To each of them, she added silently.

Maybe, just for a few days, she could pretend there were no shadows between them. Simply enjoy the *now*, and face the future when they returned to Sydney.

'Let's change and go explore the place.'

It was a large suite, with a lounge area, a spacious bedroom housing two king-size beds, and a luxurious *en suite*.

'That could be a plan,' Nic agreed with unruffled ease.

Cargo pants, Tina decided, a cotton top, and runners, filching each from her travel bag.

Sunglasses did much to shade the emerging bruise colouring her cheek, and minutes later she caught up a fun beach-hat, her camera, and preceded Nic from the suite.

The corporate executive persona disappeared as they traversed the large pool area, then began exploring the sandy beach.

He looked as relaxed as she felt. Different, she determined, intuitively aware it wasn't just his casual attire.

'Stand over there,' she directed, and held up her camera.

'You want photos?'

Memories, she accorded silently, I can take out and look at when all this is over. Something to remind me of a small slice of my life with a man who came to mean much to me.

She took several, fast, one after the other, and grinned when another couple passing by offered to take photos of them together.

It was easy to get into the act and place an arm along the back of Nic's waist. To laugh up at him when he curved his arm over her shoulders.

The laughter died as he leant down and fastened his mouth over hers in a brief, tantalising kiss...which was also recorded on celluloid.

'Thanks.' Nic took the camera and indicated the one the other couple held. 'Want me to return the favour?'

Honeymooners, Tina deduced, and couldn't help feeling envious. It must be wonderful to love and be loved, to gift up your soul to a man and receive his in return. To know there was unconditional trust.

It was easy to fall into friendly conversation for several minutes, to part with a 'see you around' comment as they went their separate ways.

Tina expected Nic to remove his arm from her shoulders, but to her surprise he left it there as they walked along the foreshore.

It was…nice. Sharing relaxed companionship, aware there were no sexual overtones.

This was what she wanted…wasn't it?

It was what she'd thought she wanted. What she'd conditioned herself to accept. Yet now she wasn't sure it was enough.

Are you insane?

This brief interlude is the last goodbye. A pleasant lead up to the moment when he'll inform me the marriage is over.

How could it be anything else?

Don't go there, a silent voice agonised.

Did Nic sense her insecurity? She hoped not.

At some point they turned and retraced their steps, re-entered their suite, showered and changed for dinner, then went down to the restaurant.

Most all of the guests wore casual gear, although some of the women had opted to dress up. It was a mixed crowd, some obvious honeymoon couples, families, maybe a stolen weekend for a few. People-watching was an interesting pastime, as long as it wasn't overt.

'How long are we staying?' Tina queried lightly as

she sipped a delicious Chardonnay between the starter and main.

'Until Sunday.'

Four days, total. A light shivery feeling raced over the surface of her skin, raising all her fine body hairs in instinctive awareness. Of the man, and the danger of being constantly in his company.

What if...?

Stop it. There is no *what if.*

But don't you want there to be? an inner voice posed.

They ordered coffee at the end of a leisurely meal, then wandered along the beach. The moon was clear, painting the ocean with a river of silver, and the faint light bathed the surroundings, etching them in varying shades of grey from palest pearl to almost black.

It was almost possible to believe in magic, Tina mused as Nic threaded his fingers through her own.

'Let's go back, shall we?'

She heard the faint drawling quality in his voice, and felt a wave of sadness roll over her. He was merely indulging her, and it hurt.

Stupid tears welled in her eyes, and she blinked rapidly to dispel them. Only to have them spill over and run slowly down each cheek.

This was crazy. What was the matter with her?

Emotional reaction, she rationalised. Let's face it, the past month hasn't exactly been a cakewalk!

She kept her head down as they entered their suite, and she missed Nic's sharp look, his slight frown. It was only when he barred her passage into the *en suite* that she became aware he'd moved across the room.

Dammit, he had the tread of a cat.

He stood close, much too close, and there was little she could do to prevent him catching hold of her chin as he tilted it towards him.

She lowered her eyelids in protective self-defence, and silently cursed the convulsive swallow of an imaginary lump in her throat.

He eased a thumb-pad over her cheek in a gentle gesture that caused another tear to spill.

'Suppose you tell me, hmm?'

Should she even begin?

'It's easy,' Nic said quietly. 'One word after the other.'

She managed a faint smile. 'You think?'

Was there ever going to be a better time? Avoiding and evading the issue would only delay the inevitable.

Okay, so what was there to lose?

'When do you want to file for divorce?' There, she'd voiced the query that had tortured her for days.

He didn't move. 'What makes you think that's my intention?'

'Isn't it? The loss of Vasili's child negates the reason for the marriage to exist,' she managed quietly. 'You'll want to be free to choose someone else.' This was becoming more difficult by the minute. 'Have children of your own.' She was grasping for words and the courage to continue. 'Provide the Leandros heir.'

He was too quiet. Dangerously so, and it unnerved her.

'You perceive that to be a logical solution?'

'Don't you?' she demanded, sorely tried.

'It would be inconceivable I might want to remain married to you?'

'Why?' she asked baldly. 'To keep the female predators at bay?'

'That, too.'

'And children? How do you propose to have them?'

A faint smile tugged the edge of his mouth. 'The usual method.'

Dear Lord in heaven…make love with him? 'You can't be serious.'

'Very serious.'

It solved the divorce, a financial settlement…a child and heir, children.

'You're wrong,' Nic offered softly as he read and defined each fleeting expression. 'On all counts.'

'Then…*why*?' The demand came out as an agonised plea.

'Because of this.' He pulled her in and fastened his mouth over hers in a kiss that took hold of her heart and sent it soaring high.

A deep, frankly sensual taking like nothing she'd experienced before. Hungry, compelling, it almost blew her mind.

He took her tentative response and led her towards something more, stoking her hunger until there was only the man and an electrifying emotion so intense it threatened to spontaneously combust.

Nic brought her down slowly, softening his touch until his mouth merely brushed hers, then he drew back a little.

'You want to deny what we share?' he queried gently.

She was almost trembling, and he stroked light fingers down her uninjured cheek.

Tina closed her eyes, then let her lashes sweep open.

'I'm not very good at this.' Let's face it, my one foray into intimacy was a disaster.

He caught her chin between thumb and forefinger. 'Do you trust me?'

She gave him a haunted look, one that took hold of his heart and squeezed a little.

'It's not fair,' she managed at last. 'If I ask you to stop.'

Nic brushed his lips to her forehead. 'Let's meet that when and if it happens.'

His mouth was gentle as it covered hers, subtly coaxing in a way that made her want more, and she wound her arms around his neck and leaned in, savouring his touch as he slid one hand down to cup her bottom while the other captured her nape.

A faint groan of protest emerged from her throat as he let his mouth trail to the sensitive cord at the edge of her neck, and sensation speared through her body as he traced the soft indentations, the hollows at the base of her throat, before edging lower.

She wanted to touch him, explore his naked flesh, caress him as he caressed her. Except he was wearing too many clothes, and she tugged at his shirt, freeing it from the waistband of his jeans, and he drew back a little and pulled the shirt over his head.

'Your turn.' He gave her no time to think as he took hold of the hem and tugged off her top. A deft movement and her bra followed.

With incredible gentleness he caressed each peak until they burgeoned beneath his touch, and she gasped out loud as he lowered his head and took one peak into his mouth and suckled there.

Dear heaven. She felt her body tremble as he moved to render a similar supplication to its twin, and she arched involuntarily to allow him easier access.

His hands travelled lower and dealt with the fastener at her waist, then he slid her jeans down and held her as she stepped out of them.

A lacy black thong was all that separated her from total nudity, and he shucked off his own jeans, then caught her close.

Not before the sight of him fully aroused captured her attention. For a moment she couldn't breathe, then she gasped as his fingers traced the lacy brief to her groin and slid beneath the silk.

She couldn't think as he teased the sensitive clitoris, and she groaned out loud as sensation spiralled through her body, all-consuming, electric.

He didn't stop, and just when she thought she'd *die* he began an intimate exploration that had her biting her lip in an effort to maintain some vestige of control.

Tina was hardly aware of Nic sweeping aside the bedcovers, or of being drawn down onto the bed.

He took his time, using his mouth, his hands, to bring her to climax, and she sobbed out loud as she went high…so high she caught hold of him and held on.

This, *this* was the emotion lyrics attempted to capture, together with poets and masters of every language.

She closed her eyes and let her breathing settle, her heart slow a little from its racing beat.

Except he was far from done.

Slowly and with infinite care, he entered her, feeling the silken tissues expand to accommodate him, and he covered her mouth with his own, absorbing the way her breath hitched, her soundless gasp as he eased back a little, then slid forward in gentle rocking movements until he reached the hilt.

Then he began to move, slowly at first, each thrust a little deeper until she caught his rhythm, matched it, and he let go of control as she soared with him, teetered at the brink, then fell with him in a climax that shattered them both.

Nic buried his mouth in the curve of her neck and held her close. His heartbeat matched hers, strong, fast, until it settled, and he felt her body quiver as he lightly traced her hip, the length of her thigh, before sliding up to cup her breast.

Afterwards Tina had no idea how long they lay entwined together, only that it felt good. Better than good. Right now she couldn't think of an adequate word in description.

At some stage they rose from the bed and took a leisurely shower, indulging in a slow, intimate exploration that led to an erotic coupling and the release of some of her inhibitions.

Towelled dry, Nic drew her down onto the bed and within minutes she slid into a dreamless sleep from which she didn't stir until the pre-dawn hours.

There was something incredibly sensually satisfying in feeling the slight pull of inner muscles, the sensation of having been possessed by a man and loved well, Tina reflected as she stretched a little and attempted to slip from the bed.

Except the arm at her waist tightened, and a warm, seeking mouth caressed the sensitive hollow at the edge of her nape.

'Where do you think you're going?'

'To make coffee, then ravish you.'

Nic's husky laughter sounded low in his throat as he turned her to face him. Dark eyes gleamed close to her own as he rolled onto his back. 'Skip the coffee.'

She was an apt pupil, he mused, who delighted him at every turn. A tentative lover, shy, and intensely fascinating.

'Are you just going to lie there?'

'If you need help,' he drawled. 'Just ask.'

This was no practised partner skilled in the art of gifting pleasure, who mostly faked each manoeuvre and sighed on learned cue.

This woman, his wife, delighted in discovering each indentation, hollow, muscle ridge, and displayed genuine enjoyment at each hitch of his breath, each groan as she lingered a little longer, teased a sensitive exploration of his penis, and the swollen pouches beneath.

She was having fun, and she gave a wicked chuckle as he pulled her on top of him and slid his hands up to her breasts.

'Now let's see how brave you are, hmm?'

'What do you call this?' she queried huskily. 'The early morning ride?'

He proceeded to show her, and it was she who cried out and held on. She, who almost collapsed as she lay sobbing against him at the extent of emotion she'd experienced.

'Enough,' Nic said gently as he traced a soothing pattern down her spine. 'Sleep a little, hmm? We have the day to explore the resort.'

Tina woke late to find Nic had already showered and dressed as he sat in the adjoining lounge reading the day's newspaper.

He glanced up as he heard her move from the bed, and the sensual warmth evident in his smile made her want to sit down again. 'Breakfast?'

She checked her watch and grimaced a little. 'Don't you mean lunch?'

'Go dress,' he bade easily. 'Then we'll eat and decide what we're going to do with the afternoon.'

CHAPTER TWELVE

THE ensuing three days numbered among the happiest in Tina's life.

At Nic's insistence, she took in relaxation therapy, visited the masseuse, had a manicure and enjoyed a session with the hairdresser.

Together they went wind-surfing, hired a catamaran, and played tennis.

The nights were something else as they drew out the anticipation by lingering over the evening meal, taking a walk along the beach, or the paths surrounding the resort itself.

All it took was an exchanged look, a touch of the hand, a murmured word, and they returned to their suite to indulge in a long, sweet loving that reached the heights and beyond in a magical, sensual world uniquely their own.

If *this* is happiness, Tina mused, why would she think of giving it up?

Anything seemed possible. A lasting marriage, children, a contented and fulfilling life with a man she adored.

What more could any woman ask?

It wasn't until they landed in Sydney late Sunday evening that a few doubts began to surface.

A return to Sydney meant a return to routine, work, a busy lifestyle.

Steve remained in residence, and with Sabine out on bail the woman was a looming spectre they couldn't afford to ignore.

'Hey, you look…incredible,' Lily pronounced when Tina arrived at the boutique. 'Bruise is something else, but the swelling has subsided. So,' she cajoled with a wicked grin. 'How was your break?'

'Really great.'

'That's it?'

She met Lily's teasing gaze and tilted her head to one side. 'What do you want me to say?'

'Oh…just, Nic was fantastic, it was the honeymoon you never had, the sex was off the Richter scale.' She offered an irrepressible grin. 'Stuff like that.'

'You're not going to give it up, are you?'

'Only if I have to.'

'Yes,' Tina said simply, and laughed as Lily executed a mock swoon. 'You're incorrigible, do you know that?'

'Of course. But we're friends…we walk the walk and talk the talk. It's what girls *do*.'

'There's the door buzzer,' Tina managed, and watched Lily morph into a serene, helpful salesperson as she turned towards the client.

It was a good day, Tina reflected as it reached time to close up and go home. Sales had been steady, expected stock arrived on time, both she and Lily had managed a reasonable lunch break, and she'd set up a stunning display for the front window.

Business was on track, and after four days of rest and relaxation she felt refreshed and vital again. True, there were moments of sadness and guilt. For the loss of a good friend in Vasili, the loss of his child, and for Stacey and Paul, to whom the child would have meant so much.

Steve entered the boutique just as she was ready to lock up, and minutes later he accompanied her to the four-wheel drive, saw her seated, then followed her home.

Nic's Lexus was in the garage when she drove in, and she ran lightly upstairs to their suite, deposited her laptop and bag, then she stripped off her clothes and walked naked into his shower.

'Well, now,' Nic drawled as she slid her arms round his neck and pulled his head down to hers for a soul-destroying kiss. 'That's some greeting.' He cupped her face between his hands and leant in. 'Want to try for a repeat?'

Her witching smile melted his heart. 'Mmm, what about dinner?'

'Dinner can wait.' With those few words he lifted her high against him and curved her thighs over his hips.

'But you can't,' Tina teased, loving the way he moved against her, the touch of his hands, his lips. Everything about him.

As long as he lived, he'd never get enough of her. Her generosity of spirit, her gift of giving so much of herself. It almost made him feel afraid.

Dinner was something they went down to the kitchen for around ten, fed each other morsels, washed it down with superb red wine, then returned to bed...this time to sleep.

Nic's breathing soon settled into a deep rhythm while Tina lapsed into contemplative thought.

A week ago she'd have given anything to have reached this level of understanding, trust and intimacy.

It was the realisation of her deepest dreams. Something she'd thought she would never achieve.

How had they come so far, so fast?

Don't analyse it, she admonished silently. Just accept life as it is.

Which was fine. She could do that. Except there was a part of her that longed for it all.

Love…the everlasting kind.

To *know*, deep in her heart, her soul, that what Nic felt for her was love, not lust.

Was that asking too much?

'I gather I'm meant to impress,' Tina teased as Nic negotiated inner city traffic.

'You manage to do that without any effort at all.'

His tolerant response held a musing drawl, and she sent him a brilliant smile.

'A compliment. How nice.'

She'd taken considerable effort with her appearance, taming her hair into a smooth knot with a few escaping tendrils framing her face. The Saab gown was a masterpiece in soft floral silk chiffon, draped bodice with spaghetti straps. Understated make-up with emphasis on her eyes, the pink gloss colouring her lips, and jewellery was a favoured diamond drop pendant and matching earrings. A light touch of perfume with floral tones added a final touch.

It was a mild spring evening, the sky a clear indigo with a soft sprinkling of pinprick stars. Soon the days would lengthen with the advent of seasonal summer, becoming more noticeable as daylight saving crept into the mix.

Sydney was a beautiful city, with its harbour, many coves and inlets, notable landmarks. Bright flashing neon signs, street lights, lit shop windows. The constant ebb and flow of city life…the good, the bad and the ugly, as it was with cities anywhere in the world.

Tonight's event was a formal dinner held in honour of a high-ranking Greek government minister, whose presence in Australia was designed to bolster trade between the two countries.

The venue was a major inner city hotel, and six-thirty for seven meant a steady stream of guests converging in the ballroom lobby as they sipped champagne.

Nic's presence created an effect among several of the women, and while some were circumspect, others were more blatant in their interest.

'Ah, there you are,' a vaguely familiar voice greeted, and Tina turned to see Eleni and Dimitri welcoming them into their circle of friends.

'Tina, so beautiful as always.' Eleni did the air-kiss thing, then caught hold of Tina's hands as she conducted a searching appraisal. 'My dear, your face. Is that a bruise? What happened?'

And there she was, thinking she'd done a great job with the concealer! 'I ran into something a few days ago.' The force of a feminine hand bent on inflicting damage, she added silently.

Eleni looked askance of Nic. 'An unfortunate accident,' he confirmed in carefully measured tones.

'Of course, an accident,' Eleni concurred with the knowledge of one who knew it couldn't possibly be anything else.

Tina decided to have a little fun, and she tucked a hand in his, then offered Nic a wistful, adoring smile. 'We've decided to delete that particular move from our—' she paused deliberately '—repertoire, haven't we, darling?'

Would he run with this and play?

He lifted their joined hands to his lips in a gesture that reduced her bones to water. 'Definitely.'

The look on Eleni's face was priceless.

'I've shocked her,' Tina said with a tinge of remorse as Eleni murmured an excuse and led Dimitri to greet a fellow guest.

'Doubtful,' Nic drawled, and gave her a quizzical look. 'Repertoire?'

'It sounded good.'

'Remind me to take you to task.'

'Can I count on that?' She sobered a little. 'Maybe I should go touch up my face.'

'The bruise is barely noticeable.'

Except Eleni had picked up on it, and Tina drew her hand free from his. 'I'll be back.'

He followed her slender frame as she threaded her way through the mingling guests, and stood outside as she entered the powder-room.

Was he being over-protective? Without doubt. He'd yet to relay Steve was staying on, combining bodyguard duties with those of general factotum.

Wealth and a high profile lifted the stakes for hostage situations, kidnapping of children, and worse.

Sensible precautions had become a fact of life.

Tina emerged within minutes and she merely lifted both eyebrows as he fell into step at her side.

Guests were already moving into the dining-room, and the evening began on time, with introductory speeches, some light entertainment in between the various courses, followed by a lengthy and detailed address by the Greek foreign minister.

The surprise of the evening came when Nic was called to the podium, and Tina watched in fascination as he delivered a flawless speech detailing the benefits of trade to both Australia and Greece, then proceeded to cite examples.

He stood perfectly at ease, and didn't refer to notes.

There was a round of applause, and as he descended from the stage he was swamped...yes, *swamped* was the right word, Tina mused, by a few society doyennes, a photographer and journalist.

'You didn't tell me,' she murmured as he returned to their table.

'It was a last-minute request. The corporate CEO scheduled to speak was unexpectedly rushed to hospital this afternoon.'

He'd come up with such a superb speech in something like an hour or so? 'I'm impressed.'

His smile held a degree of amusement. 'Thank you.'

'Yet another of your talents.' It was a genuine compliment, and he lifted a hand and brushed light fingers over her lips.

'We'll leave soon.'

It took a while. Coffee was served, and the guests began to move from table to table as the evening drew to a close.

Nic garnered attention as several fellow guests took time to offer praise, and he handled it with effortless charm.

Tina smiled a lot as she stood at his side, although the smile became a little fixed as a few of the women elected to show their enthusiasm with affection. No air-kisses there!

'Nic's new bride,' one woman guest trilled with obsequious gaiety…brought on, Tina guessed, by a little too much wine. 'Who'd have thought?'

'That I'd be a bride?' Tina queried politely. 'Or that Nic would marry me?'

'Oh, my dear, *no*. I mean of course who'd have thought Nic would *marry*?' There was that laugh again. 'I mean, he's such a catch. You must tell me your secret.'

It was too much for Tina. 'Sex,' she revealed with a very straight, even, earnest expression. 'Lots and lots of sex.'

The woman's eyes almost crossed as she made a valiant attempt at recovery. 'Really?'

Tina's expression remained unchanged. 'Yes,' she managed quietly. *'Really.'*

'You do realise,' Nic drawled much later as he eased the car into the flow of traffic, 'your musing banter will be circulated among the social set.'

'And that's a problem?' She shook her head. 'What it is to have earned a reputation.' She sighed, and sent him a sideways glance. 'Your wild sexual animal meter will go right through the roof,' she mocked lightly.

He laughed, a low, husky sound that liquefied her bones.

'Perhaps you should give it a test run.'

'I live to please,' she assured him solemnly.

And she did please him. As she helped divest him of his clothes after first shedding her own. As she pushed him down onto the bed and played the vamp.

Yet as she drove him wild it was he who took control and led her on a journey of discovery along a path she'd never travelled before.

Just as she thought it couldn't become more magical, he took her higher, until she cried out and begged for his possession.

It was wicked sorcery at its peak. Unrestrained, and transcending mere passion. A raw, primitive hunger that tore at the heart, the soul, and left them each sheened with sensual heat, breathless from the force of what they'd just shared.

Lust, Tina accorded on the edge of sleep.

But *what about love*?

CHAPTER THIRTEEN

'SPECIAL delivery for Tina Leandros.'

Tina glanced up from the client she was attending, murmured an apology, crossed to the counter, signed the proffered clipboard and cast the attractive gift-box a puzzled look.

Nic? Claire? She couldn't think of anyone else who might send an unexpected gift.

The morning was busy, so much so Lily transferred the box into the back room where it remained untouched for several hours. Lunch came and went, and it was almost mid-afternoon before Tina had a chance to check it out.

Beautiful wrapping, she mused as she slid off the elaborate bow. No visible card. Probably tucked inside somewhere.

Lots of tissue paper. Her fingers parted it all as she dug in deep. Ah, there it was…a second small gift-wrapped box.

Jewellery?

The wrapping undid easily, and she slid open the expensive velvet case, unsure quite what to expect.

The breath caught in her throat, and her eyes widened with shock as the contents lay revealed. A miniature baby doll, naked except for a gauze nappy, with a pin piercing its heart. The accompanying card read, 'Sorry for your loss'.

Deliberately cruel, it could only have one source.

'What is it?' Lily queried with concern.

Had she uttered a strangled sound? She wasn't sure.

Lily joined her, took one look, muttered something vicious beneath her breath, caught up the phone and hit speed-dial.

'What are you doing?'

'Calling Nic.'

'Don't. He has important meetings all day.'

Lily shook her head. 'I was given specific instructions.'

'Cut the connection,' Tina insisted. 'I'll tell him tonight.' Without good cause, for Lily blithely ignored her. Seconds later she handed over the phone.

'I'm on my way.'

'There's no need—' Except Nic had already hung up.

She sent Lily a telling glare. 'Please. Do I *look* like a fragile flower?'

'I'll make some tea.'

'Enough, already,' she dismissed with very real exasperation. An emotion that was evident a short while later when Nic walked through the door.

'I'm fine,' Tina reiterated, and barely caught her breath as he pulled her in and fastened his mouth over hers in a kiss that took hold of her suspended emotions and made her temporarily forget where she was.

'Uh-huh.' His gaze searched her features, glimpsed the bruised hurt apparent in the depths of those dark emerald eyes, and brushed his lips over hers. 'We're going home.'

'I can't—'

'Lily will lock up.'

'What *is* it with you two?'

'A conspiracy.' He kissed her again, and she leaned in against him, savoured his warmth, strength, the security he offered…and so much more. 'Taking care of you,' he added quietly. 'Let's go.'

She gave an eloquent sigh that was part smile, part resignation. 'Do I have a choice?'

'No.'

The police would collect the box, wrapping and contents. Steve was already on it, as well as conducting a search of the city's delivery agents.

It was highly probable Sabine had outsmarted them by using gloves to avoid any fingerprint evidence. But the delivery was traceable…and if Sabine could be positively identified, conviction and sentencing would follow.

Not before time, he thought grimly.

Tina collected her bag, laptop and keys, and gave Lily a hug. 'Thanks. I'll see you tomorrow.'

'You go first,' Nic directed as they reached the staff car park. 'I'll follow.'

'Where?'

'Home.'

Well, there you go. *Home* had a nice ring to it. And the elegant house set in landscaped grounds *had* become home…her personal sanctuary with the man who was the love of her life.

Nic saw her seated in the four-wheel drive, then he crossed to the Lexus, waited until she eased her vehicle onto the road, and followed close behind.

Steve was in the lobby when they entered it.

'A minor breakthrough. I have the delivery firm, they're checking their staff. There's one possible, but the pick-up point doesn't match Sabine.'

'She could have used someone as a front.'

'Highly likely. I'm on it.'

Tina moved towards the stairs. A shower and a change into comfortable clothes was a priority. Afterwards she'd walk Czar, check what Maria had left for dinner, and relax.

In the suite she slid off her stilettos, stripped off her clothes and walked into the *en suite*, adjusted the temperature dial and stepped beneath the warm, pulsing water.

Heaven. She closed her eyes and let the heated spray wash over her. Any minute soon she'd scoop up the soap…but for now she'd *enjoy*.

A faint sound caused her eyes to spring open and they widened measurably as Nic stepped in to join her.

Her lips formed a witching smile, and her eyes…dear Lord, a man could drown in those brilliant emerald depths.

'You have your own bathroom,' Tina teased, and saw the indolent warmth apparent as he pulled her close.

'Sharing yours is so much more fun.'

'I'm partial to rose-scented soap.' She caught it up and ran the bar over his chest, his stomach, lower, only to have the breath hitch in her throat as he returned the favour.

'And that's a problem?'

It was a game, a delightful play by lovers, and one in which she exulted. 'It might fight with your cologne.'

'You think?' His lips nuzzled the sensitive edge of her neck, and felt her pulse kick in to a faster beat.

'Uh-huh.'

He trailed gentle fingers down the length of her spine, caressing each indentation, and felt her body quiver.

'Want me to leave?'

Her hands settled on his hips and drew him against her. His arousal was a potent force, and hers, all hers. 'Not if you value your life.'

He fastened his mouth over hers, savouring the taste and feel of her, the moist, sweet tissues, her generosity as his tongue swept hers, bit gently, then possessed in a manner that left her in no doubt as to the degree of his passion.

And matched it, wanting more, so much more, as she clung to him and held on as if she'd never let go.

'You want to take this in the bedroom?'

'What's wrong with the shower?'

A soft, husky chuckle emerged from his lips. 'It'll do for a start.'

He lifted her high and she wound her legs over his hips, then arched back a little. 'Hmm, you learn something new each day.'

Her soft laugh became a faint groan as he eased her into a gentle rocking movement, then lowered his head to her breast.

Her breath quickened as he savoured one peak, then took it into his mouth and grazed it with his teeth.

Heat surged through her veins, encompassing every nerve in her body until she was on fire, mindless in passion that demanded more, so much more than pre-coital play.

'Please.'

Yet he was far from done, and she cried out as he

used his hands to caress and stroke, stoking the fire to fever-pitch.

Then he positioned her carefully and drove deep in one slow thrust, feeling her silken body stretch to accommodate him, hold him fast, before she began to move, easily catching his rhythm and matching it, taking them both high to a place where sheer sensation ruled.

Quickened breathing and soft groans were masked by the pulsing water, and just as she began to ease back a little he took her so high she simply held on and rode the sensual storm, exulting in it, *him*, and the love they shared.

It was more, so much more than she had ever hoped to have in her life...the man, the all-consuming passion. And *love*. It took her breath away.

Nic held her close, then angled his mouth down to hers in a lingering kiss so incredibly sweet she wanted to weep from the sheer joy of it.

He was the other half of her soul. The air that she breathed. Her life.

Every day, each night, her love for him seemed to grow. Just when she thought it couldn't be *more*, it moved up another notch.

There was trust, unequivocal and enduring. All the doubts, the insecurities were gone. In its place was something so special, so unique to each of them, it brought tears to her eyes.

'Hey,' Nic chided gently. He caught hold of her chin and lifted it, then pressed a thumb to the sensitive curve of her lower lip. 'What's this?'

'You,' she said shakily, and saw his eyes flare a

little. Oh, God, there were words she wanted, *needed* to say, and she hardly knew how or where to begin.

She touched his lips, trailed light fingers across that sensual curve and held them at its edge.

The ghost of a smile shook her lips. 'I love you.' There, she'd said it. 'I never thought I could feel this way.'

She brought him undone. Totally. He cupped her face with his hands and glimpsed the naked emotion in the depths of her eyes.

'Tina.'

'Don't. Please, not yet.' She was oblivious to everything, except the man. 'There's so much...' She bit her lip, unsure where to begin.

'Vasili's baby,' she managed shakily, and trembled as he smoothed a thumb over her cheek. 'Just as I was dealing with the guilt associated with the how and why of its conception, Vasili died. The baby represented an extension of his life. I couldn't take the easy way out.' The next part was painful. 'There was Stacey and Paul,' she managed. '*You.*' A lump rose in her throat, and she swallowed it. 'Marriage as a viable solution for the child's benefit.'

Her eyes were large emerald pools as she silently begged him to let her continue. Nic smoothed away the slow trickle of tears and felt his heart clench at her visible distress.

'The pregnancy became the glue that held us together.' She faltered a little. 'A child who didn't ask to be conceived, but one who meant so much.' It hurt, but she needed to get it all out. 'When I miscarried, it wasn't only the loss of the child that upset me. It was the prospect of losing you.' Her eyes searched his. 'For without the child, there was no need for the marriage to continue.'

'Fool,' Nic chided gently.

'You were so…supportive. Caring,' she added. 'In hospital, afterwards. I wanted the affection you displayed to be real. Not just a result of misplaced duty.'

Oh, hell, this wasn't easy. 'Every day I expected you to tell me the lawyers would be called in, the marriage annulled, and we'd each go our separate ways.'

She wasn't done. 'Then when you suggested we consummate the marriage and produce our own child…' Words momentarily failed her. 'I realised it wasn't me you wanted. It was a Leandros heir.'

'When we made love…how could you not know the effect you had on me?'

Truth, honesty. If ever there was the right time for it, it was now.

'I rationalised it was just sex.' Very good sex. Right off the Richter scale. 'And you were very practised in the art of pleasing a woman.'

'And my reaction? That was due simply to *practice*? Not because of the woman I held in my arms? The way I felt for her, *loved* her?'

Tina thought her heart stopped. Everything seemed suspended…time, place.

Her voice was little more than a whisper. 'What did you say?'

'*Love*,' he reiterated quietly. 'My love for you. Only *you*.'

It was almost too much. More than she had ever hoped for, or believed she would ever have.

'The first time I laid eyes on you was across an

open grave at my brother's funeral. The solemnity and pain of the occasion, the fact you were pregnant with Vasili's child...' He took a moment, then continued, 'None of it diminished the instant attraction I instinctively fought against.'

He brushed his mouth against her own, lingered, then reluctantly drew back a little. 'You fascinated me. Your strength, unswerving loyalty. Vulnerability,' he added quietly. 'I could have torn limb from limb the man whose vicious attack almost destroyed your emotional heart.'

He watched her swallow the sudden lump that had risen in her throat, and resisted the temptation to pull her close. Soon, he vowed silently.

'I wanted you in my life. Marriage was the only option. I just had to convince you of it.'

He'd used considerable skill in achieving his objective. But then, hadn't *she* condoned the marriage for similar reasons she was unwilling to identify with at the time?

'There was a need to stand back,' Nic relayed gently. 'Allow you time to trust me.' He waited a beat. 'To trust yourself.

'I silently wept with you when you miscarried,' he continued gently. 'For what the child would have meant...to Stacey, Paul. To each of us, for much the same reasons. But for you, especially,' he added. 'As much as it was Vasili's child, it was also yours.'

They were so nearly there. Only a few loose ends remained. 'Sabine—'

Tina pressed a finger to his mouth. 'She's a beautiful seductress who became unhealthily obsessed with you.'

How could she voice what she wanted to say, and have it sound right? 'Very few people escape without accumulating some baggage in their lives. It's the way you deal with it that makes the difference.'

'She could have harmed you.' The thought had kept him awake nights, seen him carry security measures to the extreme.

'She didn't get the opportunity.'

He'd made sure of it.

'I've cleared my diary,' Nic enlightened as he dropped a kiss to the tip of her nose. 'As from Monday.' Delegated, assigned, organised with cut-throat precision. 'For a month.'

A *month*? 'You have?'

'Aren't you going to ask why?'

Her eyes gleamed with soft humour. 'Surprise me.'

'We fly out late Monday *en route* to Athens, then we'll spend a few weeks touring the Greek Islands.'

A delighted smile curved that delectable mouth. 'Santorini? I've always wanted to visit there.'

'Naturally.'

'I think I love you.'

He lowered his head to touch her forehead with his own. 'Only *think*?'

Her smile widened. 'You want a rundown on my innermost thoughts?'

'Sounds like a plan.'

His voice was light, but there was a seriousness apparent, one that sent a quivering sensation through her body.

'Don't you think we should get out of here first?'

Nic reached out and closed the water dial, then he filched a towel and began blotting the moisture from her body, loving the silky texture of her skin, the slight curves…the way she quivered at his touch.

'My turn,' Tina said gently when he was done. The flex of muscle and sinew fascinated her, the hard ridges, his tight butt. The narrow waist, washboard midriff, the strong breadth of his shoulders.

'We should get dressed.'

He skimmed his hands over her body and cupped her face. 'You think?'

Held like this, she was past thinking. 'You have a better idea?'

He drew her into the bedroom, tossed back the covers, and showed her, very thoroughly, just what it meant to be loved and adored as he led her on a sensuous witching journey that fragmented her control and turned her into a shameless wanton.

Magic, she sighed a long time later. Mesmeric, intoxicating, primitive.

'Thank you,' she said huskily from within the sanctuary of his arms.

'For what, specifically?' He pressed lips to her forehead, and was unable to resist the urge to tease a little. 'Good sex?'

'For caring, believing in me.' Having the patience to ride out the emotional storm.

'A given. As it will be for the rest of my life,' he added quietly.

'I love you.' He was everything…all she could ever wish for, and more. She had a burning need to show him how much, in a way words never could.

It took a while, and it was he who groaned beneath her touch, loving the witching siren she became as she pleasured him…until he could take no more. He didn't wait to reverse their positions, he simply caught hold of her waist, lifted her to straddle him, and proceeded to take her on the ride of her life.

Afterwards she wasn't capable of moving so much as a muscle.

Nic curved an arm round her waist and traced a finger down the slope of her nose. 'Sleepy?'

'Uh-huh.'

'I didn't thank you.' He paused imperceptibly. 'For gifting me the most precious gift of all. *You.*' Truly a gift from the heart, and one he would treasure for as long as he lived.

Eternity.

'Same goes,' Tina said quietly, smiling a little as she caught hold of his hand and pressed it to her lips.

This was one of the most precious moments of her life; she was aware there would be many more as the years unfolded.

The birth of a much-wanted child or three. Celebrations and anniversaries.

One entity would remain a constant.

Love. Theirs for each other.

The for-ever kind.

MILLS & BOON

IT TAKES A

Hero

... to sweep you off your feet.

CAROL MARINELLI SARAH MORGAN
CAROLINE ANDERSON

On sale 5th August 2005

*Available at most branches of WHSmith, Tesco, ASDA, Martins,
Borders, Eason, Sainsbury's and all good paperback bookshops.*

FREE

4 BOOKS AND A SURPRISE GIFT!

We would like to take this opportunity to thank you for reading this
Mills & Boon® book by offering you the chance to take FOUR more
specially selected titles from the Modern Romance™ series absolutely
FREE! We're also making this offer to introduce you to the benefits of
the Reader Service™—

> ★ FREE home delivery
> ★ FREE gifts and competitions
> ★ FREE monthly Newsletter
> ★ Books available before they're in the shops
> ★ Exclusive Reader Service offers

Accepting these FREE books and gift places you under no obligation
to buy; you may cancel at any time, even after receiving your free
shipment. Simply complete your details below and return the entire
page to the address below. You don't even need a stamp!

YES! Please send me 4 free Modern Romance books and a surprise
gift. I understand that unless you hear from me, I will receive 6
superb new titles every month for just £2.75 each, postage and packing
free. I am under no obligation to purchase any books and may cancel
my subscription at any time. The free books and gift will be mine to
keep in any case.

P5ZEE

Ms/Mrs/Miss/Mr.......................................Initials ....
BLOCK CAPITALS PLEASE

Surname ....

Address ....

....

....Postcode ....

Send this whole page to:

The Reader Service, FREEPOST CN81, Croydon, CR9 3WZ

Offer valid in UK only and is not available to current Reader Service™ subscribers to this series. Overseas and Eire please
write for details. We reserve the right to refuse an application and applicants must be aged 18 years or over. Only one
application per household. Terms and prices subject to change without notice. Offer expires 30th November 2005. As a
result of this application, you may receive offers from Harlequin Mills & Boon and other carefully selected companies. If
you would prefer not to share in this opportunity please write to The Data Manager at PO Box 676, Richmond, TW9 1WU.

Mills & Boon® is a registered trademark owned by Harlequin Mills & Boon Limited.
Modern Romance™ is being used as a trademark. The Reader Service™ is being used as a trademark.